On the Shoulders of Giants

The public promotion of diverse books through the We Need Diverse Books campaign has added to the awareness of the need to promote, teach, and research books by all types of diverse authors and about a wide range of diverse characters. Within this book series we will survey and discuss the history of African American Authors of Young Adult Literature.

We separate this history into three, two decade periods beginning in 1960. The first book covers the first wave of what we classify as three waves of African American Young Adult Literature. In the 1960s and into the 1980s, the production of books by and about African Americans in the Young Adult classification was slim. The first book covers the first wave; which we consider the ground breaking work of four pioneers: Virginia Hamilton, Walter Dean Myers, Mildred Taylor, and Julius Lester.

The second wave, covered in the second book of the series, consists of a group of authors who began writing in the late 1980s. This group consists of eight authors who expanded the foundation and built a critical reputation that garnered a variety of nominations and awards. These authors are: Rita Williams-Garcia, Jacqueline Woodson, Angela Johnson, Nikki Grimes, Sharon Draper, Christopher Paul Curtis, and Sharon G. Flake, and Jewel Parker Rhodes.

A few of these authors also write children's books, but their major contributions are in the area of middle grades or young adult literature. They are, without question, the major contributors during this time period. There are several other authors who have a large catalogue of children's book who also have one or two young adult novels, but their reputation rests squarely in the category of children's literature.

Given the growth of young adult literature from the 1980 and through the beginning years of the 21st century, some would find it strange that only 12 authors, four in the first wave and 8 in the second wave carry the reputation of African American Young Adult Literature. Yet, this is the case. Other authors also wrote books that would be considered young adult literature, but they were either not well received or not adequately promoted. There are others who have major reputations as traditional adult authors whose works are actively read by adolescents, but are not authors of Young Adult Literature.

For example, Harlem Renaissance authors are often taught in schools but they are hardly writers of young adult fiction. Others, Ralph Ellison, Richard Wright, James Baldwin, Zora Neale Hurston, Lorraine Hansberry, Nikki Giovanni, Gwendolyn Brooks, and August Wilson all have a presence in middle and high school curricula, and these author are African American representatives in the traditional canon. More contemporary African American artist are also read by adolescents; Toni Morrison, Alice Walker, Rita Dove, and Walter Mosley, but again their target audience is much older.

The third book covers the third wave and paves the path into the 21st century. Without a doubt, there is an abundance of authors writing and establishing a literary reputation. In this section, we highlight eight authors who began publishing in the 21st century and have garnered awards and significant literary reputations in a relatively short period of time. These authors are Andrea Davis Pinkney, Shelia P. Moses, Coe Booth, Kwame Alexander, Kekla Magoon, Varian Johnson, Renee Watson and Jason Reynolds. There are others that deserve to be read and watched, but the situation remains that, at this point in time, these authors have separated themselves from the rest. They are writing with more variety, more genres and stronger voices.

On the Shoulders of Giants

Celebrating African American Authors of Young Adult Literature

Edited by Steven T. Bickmore and
Shanetia P. Clark

ROWMAN & LITTLEFIELD
Lanham • Boulder • New York • London

Published by Rowman & Littlefield
A wholly owned subsidiary of The Rowman & Littlefield Publishing Group, Inc.
4501 Forbes Boulevard, Suite 200, Lanham, Maryland 20706
www.rowman.com

Unit A, Whitacre Mews, 26-34 Stannary Street, London SE11 4AB

British Library Cataloguing in Publication Information Available

Library of Congress Cataloging-in-Publication Data

Library of Congress Control Number: 2019952086

ISBN 978-1-4758-4352-1 (cloth)
ISBN 978-1-4758-4353-8 (paper)
ISBN 978-1-4758-4354-5 (electronic)

Contents

Foreword

KaaVonia Hinton

Dr. Rudine Sims Bishops's African American Children's Literature was my favorite class when I studied English education at the Ohio State University. I still have the course pack, which included essays by two of the authors highlighted in this book, Virginia Hamilton and Mildred D. Taylor. A significant member of my dissertation committee, I cannot imagine attempting to study African American Young Adult (AAYA) literature—texts by and about blacks—without Dr. Bishop's guidance.

I was thrilled when Steven T. Bickmore and Shanetia P. Clark, young adult literature scholars, asked me to write the foreword for this important book about AAYA, a book that recognizes the impact Dr. Bishop has made on the field and by allowing budding scholars like me to stand on *her* shoulders. Each of the authors featured in this volume were mentioned in Dr. Bishop's chapter, "The Image-Makers," in her seminal book, *Shadow & Substance: Afro-American Experience in Contemporary Children's Fiction* (1982).

Over thirty-five years ago, Dr. Bishop praised Virginia Hamilton, Walter Dean Myers, and Mildred D. Taylor, in particular, for their focus on "the positive aspects of Afro-American experience—the good times, the idea that the love and the support of family, friends, and community can 'prop you up on every leaning side' . . . [and] emphasize . . . the individual strengths and the inner resources that enable us to cope and to survive" (p. 96).

As this volume makes clear, these authors' influence and importance has only increased since Dr. Bishop made this statement, a statement that should not be viewed as hyperbole. I have written that during my own adolescence growing up in rural North Carolina, AAYA was influential. When my 8th-grade teacher taught Taylor's *Roll of Thunder, Hear My Cry*, it made me realize "that regardless of my socioeconomic status, my race, or my gender,

I have a place in this world and the potential to make a positive contribution to society" (p. 285).

AAYA has the power to be agentic, and the chapters in this book echo this sentiment. The chapters also argue that using literature to affirm black readers and to provide varied images of black life to all students is essential. In the pages of this book, Bickmore and Clark have assembled chapters that focus on the purpose and longevity of the Coretta Scott King Award, which makes books like the ones discussed here visible; examine important themes in AAYA; and discuss how Virginia Hamilton, Walter Dean Myers, Julius Lester, and Mildred D. Taylor produced work that "liberated" readers.

In Clark and Bickmore's chapter, they mention Hamilton's term "Liberation Literature," which she defined as "the literature of trial and struggle to freedom, through which the reader bears witness to the tribulation and ultimate deliverance, thus becoming liberated as well" (p. XII). The voices in this book emphasize that Hamilton, Myers, Lester, and Taylor are foundational authors who have written powerful texts about racial, social, and cultural issues that can be taken up using any number of lenses from reception theory, critical multiculturalism, and whiteness studies to biocriticism and critical race theory.

I, and the chapter authors, believe these works should not be relegated to Black History Month or to an annual multicultural unit. Instead, these books should be integrated throughout the curriculum during the school year. This can be done with ease using the numerous meaningful, creative, and engaging strategies (e.g., storytelling, performance, visual art, and music) suggested by the authors for individuals, small groups, and whole classrooms.

Recently, Karen Chandler (in press) noted how exciting it is that there are a number of new AAYA writers being recognized by award panels, readers, teachers, and scholars but also lamented that many works by AAYA greats are going out of print. This edited volume expresses a similar concern and brings much needed attention to these foundational authors so they can be read in conversation with contemporary books by authors such as Ibi Zoboi, Jason Reynolds, and Kekla Magoon.

As I read these chapters by well-established scholars of YA literature, I became excited because this book is a valuable tool a new generation of prospective and practicing teachers can use to help their own students be inspired by literary giants who created and shaped the AAYA field, yet remain relevant today. There are still too few books such as this one, and I for one will be shelving it right beside two other important edited volumes on the topic: Karen Smith's *African-American Voices in Young Adult Literature: Tradition, Transition, Transformation* (1996); and Wanda Brooks and Jonda McNair's *Embracing, Evaluating and Examining African American Children's and Young Adult Literature* (2008).

REFERENCES

Bishop, R. S. (1982). *Shadow and substance: Afro-American experience in contemporary children's fiction.* Illinois: National Council of Teachers of English.

Brooks W. & J. McNair, Eds. (2008). *Embracing, evaluating and examining African American children's and young adult literature.* Lanham, MD: Scarecrow Press.

Chandler, K. (2019) Uncertain directions in Black children's literature. *Lion and the Unicorn*, vol. 43, pp. 172–181.

Hamilton, V. (1992). Foreword. In A. L. Manna & C. S. Brodie (Ed.), *Many faces, many voices, multicultural literary experiences for youth: The Virginia Hamilton conference* (pp. XI–XIII). Fort Atkinson, WI: Highsmith Press.

Hinton, K., & Berry, T. (2004). Literacy, literature, and diversity. *Journal of Adolescent and Adult Literacy, 48*(4), 284–288.

Smith, K. P. (1994). *African-American voices in young adult literature: Tradition, transition, transformation.* Metuchen, NJ: Scarecrow Press.

Preface

Shanetia P. Clark

This volume has been a labor of love. Steve shared his idea of the project of collection centered around African American young adult authors as we walked to the exhibit hall at the NCTE annual convention in St. Louis, Missouri. I was "all in" immediately, and I told him that I wanted to support the project in any way possible. My excitement about the possibilities of the project surged. Later, our conversations evolved into the two of us coediting this volume and series.

Steve and I strive for this coedited collection to celebrate the pioneers of African American authors of young adult literature. Our aim for this volume, as well as the whole series, is to serve as resource for classroom teachers, teacher educators, reading specialists, librarians, and other educators who are in the field of studying, researching, teaching, and reading young adult literature. We want this book to supplement studies in the foundations of African American authors of young adult literature and explorations of critical works by these authors.

We acknowledge that many African American authors and genres could have been the spotlight in this volume. However, this book focuses on the works of Walter Dean Myers, Virginia Hamilton, Julius Lester, and Mildred D. Taylor. We asked colleagues and other scholars who should be included in this specific volume, and these four names were uplifted the most often. Therefore, we concluded that this volume will focus on the cornerstones of African American authors of young adult literature.

With these authors are our anchor, Steve and I selected a structure of the book. The first two chapters of the book discussed the history and the impact of the Coretta Scott King Book Awards on the world of YA literature. Following that first chapter, I provide an overview of the themes and critical foundations found in the work of these four authors and the continued need for more books and greater access to these books in the lives of adolescents.

We then have two distinct sections. The next four chapters—one for each author that surveys their work, their accolades, and how audiences initially responded to their work—situate the highlighted authors' early works. Each chapter highlights a single work and discusses how it might be taught: providing pre-, during-, and post-reading activities. In some cases, the chapter authors provide individual, small-group, or whole-class activities. Activities structured are then left to the discretion of the teacher as to when to place them in relationship to reading and teaching the book.

The second section is similar in structure but focuses on how the author is treated and discussed today. Each chapter within this section unpacks a work by the author and then discusses how it is used today. Some of the guiding questions that anchor the reception of the authors' work today included: Is it ignored? Has it become part of a recognized canon? Is it frequently included in classroom curricula? Can it be readily found in the library? Finally, at the end of each chapter, the author outlines activities inspired by a young adult literature text written by Myers, Hamilton, Lester, or Taylor. These included pre-, during-, and post-reading activities that can be implemented in individual, small-group, or whole-class formats.

To conclude this volume, Steve and I discuss the legacy, the reputation, the enduring impact of these authors on young adult literature. We discuss the potential ways these authors are ignored and how they have been held up as models for succeeding generations of African American authors. We claim they are giants in the field and in the world of young adult literature. Their influence is substantial, their works remain important, and a failure to continue to discuss them would be tragic.

Introduction

Steven T. Bickmore

What youthful mother, a shape upon her lap
Honey of generation had betrayed,
And that must sleep, shriek, struggle to escape
As recollection or the drug decide,
Would think her son, did she but see that shape
With sixty or more winters on its head,
A compensation for the pang of his birth,
Or the uncertainty of his setting forth?
  Among School Children by W. B. Yeats (1989)

I awoke recently with the memory of a dream. These flashbacks seem to be happening more frequently as I inch closer to the end of a forty plus year career in education. I remembered a poem—"Among School Children." It seemed fitting for my mood and for my quest to finish, what I consider to be a very important project. I do sit "with sixty or more winters" as I worry into completion a project in which this book is the first of three.

It started several years ago as I contemplated my role as an ally in the promotion of and research in diverse Young Adult (YA) literature. What do I have to say? Is it my place to say it? Is the right time? If not now, when? I began by imagining a book that would explain, explicate, and promote the work of the few recognized African American writers of YA from the birth of this classification in the late 1960 to the current burgeoning field of YA. A field that now boasts more promising African American writers than ever before.

Many current readers and younger academics are gleefully waiting for the new books by the likes of Nic Stone, Angie Thomas, Tiffany Jackson, Varian Jones, Jason Reynolds, Ibi Zoboi, Toni Adeyemi, Jay Coles, Sherri L. Smith, Dhonielle Clayton, Kwame Alexander, Nikki Grimes, or Lamar Giles. The fact that many readers can think of even more contemporary African American authors in a variety of genres speaks to the growth of the field. Yet, in comparison, the number of diverse books published each year is still woefully out of balance. Fifty years ago, not only was the ratio worse, the number of African American authors who had a significant body of work that was published by a major house could be counted on one hand.

Shanetia and I began planning the book. We scoured lists, old awards, and asked older scholars if we were missing anybody. We wanted to focus on authors who had made a significant contribution to the body of YA literature. Who has more than a couple of books? Who has won a major award? Whose books are still in print? There were more African American authors with significant contributions in children's literature than compared to YA. A few authors had a single book that might be considered middle grades or YA by today's definition. Our point, however, was to focus on those writers who carried the weight in the early years. Especially, considering how their work influences the field today.

In our conversations with other scholars, librarians, and those in the field, some names continued to rise to the surface. Most of them also wrote children's literature, yet those of us who study YA literature, recognize the names of Virginia Hamilton, Walter Dean Myers, Mildred Taylor, and Julius Lester as giants in the field. Not only did they contribute works during the first twenty years of the expansion of YA, most wrote over a forty- to fifty-year span. This grouping of authors was, indeed, small, but the quality of their work was significant.

It is still remarkable to us that from 1967 to 1987, these *are* the African American writers that were available, won awards, and were featured and promoted by publishers. Were they the only ones writing? Were they the only ones capable of writing? Definitely not. Yet, it seems that during this period, these writers were the ones that were gaining notice. They carried the weight of representing their community, of being *the* African American YA author. It was as if those making publication decisions weren't searching for more authors who produced "own voices" texts or diverse books by this portion of society. While their work is significant, it represents only the slimmest of slices of YA books available.

The renowned scholar Rudine Sims Bishop discussed this slight in representation and its effect on children. Her seminal essay, "Mirrors, Windows, and Sliding Doors" (1990), examines the essential need for children to see themselves in books and, equally as important, for children in the majority to see children who are not *them* in significant roles in books as well. Indeed, to see them in the real lives they inhabit. It was a direct call for diverse books that predates the #WeNeedDiverseBooks movement by twenty years.

Sharon Draper, a writer we consider part of the second wave of African American writers, with her first publication in 1994, told me that she never saw herself in books (personal communication, June 5, 2015). She read widely—Nancy Drew, Trixie Belden, and others—but she wasn't there. Later, as a teacher, she didn't find enough books that represented her students, who were also members of diverse populations; so, she wrote one. And then another and another and the world of literature is richer for her contributions. Her experience is representative of the vast number of African American children growing up in the United States.

As a white male, I saw and see myself all the time in books. Remarkably, it also happened to be the books that provided windows to other lives that struck me as memorable. I knew just a bit about being "othered," however. As the only Mormon is my 2nd-grade classroom in El Paso, Texas, I remember that first call for silent prayers.

I dutifully folded my arms, bowed my head, and waited for someone to pray. I became the object of attention as everyone else (or so it seemed) genuflected and then turned to see what I was doing. I was lost; I had never seen this before. I was the odd man out. Daily, I watched as they, seemingly in unison, waved their hands and I held mine motionless in a tight folded posture.

What was the impact of this event? It was fifty-five years ago and every time I hear someone generically deride Muslims, I remember. When talk of prayer in public schools surfaces, I remember. I wonder how marginalized a child might feel in a classroom that expects a certain response to a specific request that might involve their religious beliefs or practices.

Often the child is expected to perform in a predictable way, yet she legitimately has no clue what to do. Then, I imagine the incident compounded, by language, race, culture, and ethnicity. Hopefully, I have been kinder. At the same time, I know that my own childhood and adolescence were full of the racist comment, the improper joke, and the failure to include someone.

Few things are as humbling as sitting at dinner with Sharon Draper and Sharon Flake, especially if you have asked them to educate you about being a white scholar trying to look critically at diversity in YA literature. They are both forthright and will be direct. I try, but my experience will be lacking—always and forever.

I remember reading *The Contender* (Lipsyte, 1967) as an adolescent shortly after it was published. It was wonderful, vibrant, and engaging. I felt I was learning about the life of a black urban adolescents. Well, I was. But it was not the voice of an insider. I still love Lipsyte's story. It is powerful, has craftsmanship, and still engages the kids who find it.

I believe Lipstye would be one of the first to value the work and contributions of Taylor, Hamilton, Lester, and Myers and the rest of the authors we salute in the next two volumes. We will probably never be able to answer the questions posed in this introduction concerning who else should have been included during those early years of YA literature. It remains a gap in the research. Certainly, there were others writing and trying to find their way in the publishing world and further research might uncover who they were and what they were writing.

REFERENCES

Bishop, R. S. (1990). Mirrors, windows, and sliding glass doors. *Perspectives: Choosing and Using Books for the Classroom, 6*(3), ix–xi.
Lipsyte, R. (1967). *The contender*. New York: Harper & Row.
Yeats, W. B. (1989). Among school children by William Butler Yeats. Retrieved from https://www.poetryfoundation.org/poems/43293/among-school-children. June 25, 2019.

Part I

CRITICAL FOUNDATION, ESTABLISHED THEMES, AND RECEPTION OF AFRICAN AMERICAN AUTHORS

Chapter 1

Looking Back to Move Forward

A Retrospective of the Coretta Scott King Award

Deborah Taylor

The Coretta Scott King Book Awards were established in 1969 to provide recognition for African American authors—and later, illustrators—of books for children and teen readers. Two librarians, Glyndon Flynt Greer and Mabel McKissick, and publisher John Carroll observed at that time that "no African American author or illustrator had ever been honored with the prestigious Newbery and Caldecott awards." Indeed, a notable absence.

These two awards represented the hallmark of children's publishing and served to provide recognition in the field and to inspire the creators of such work. It was thought that an award recognizing outstanding work by African Americans would bring "more attention" to the fine work they were creating, thus the birth of the Coretta Scott King Book Award.

It is striking that the two librarian founders worked in schools and understood, first hand, the importance of students seeing themselves in quality books would have in the classroom and in the lives of children and adolescents. The role of formal education as a pathway to success in society was a key component in the Civil Rights Movement and remains critical in guiding thoughts about African American life.

As we have reached fifty years of this prestigious award, it is interesting to see how far children's publishing has come, or not, in spotlighting books by African American writers and artists. Certainly, there have been some improvements. More books by African American writers demonstrate their appeal with time on bestseller lists.

Deborah Taylor explained in a conversation with winners and committee members who have been part of the influential children's book awards about the trend prior to the Coretta Scott King Award:

I was a young adult librarian in the early to mid-1970s, and I worked in a
majority-African-American community. If there were books about race, they
were about the "Negro problem," so to speak, never by anyone actually growing
up and living through those experiences. You could find an occasional biography, but there was not a lot. And many of the books that were about African-
American life were not written by African Americans. A little bit later, we
started to get books by Walter Dean Myers, and things like [Mildred Taylor's]
Roll of Thunder, Hear My Cry. (Ford, 2019)

This chapter explores the Coretta Scott King Book Award over the decades
since its inception and its place in the past, present, and future of literature
for children's and YA literature. In each of the decades that make up the fifty
years of the award, the selections tell us something about the state of children's and young people's publishing and the role African Americans played.
Additionally, the books selected in each decade provide some insight into
the issues faced by the awards committee as they attempted to fulfill their
mission.

THE 1970s

The books to receive recognition during the first decade of the Coretta Scott
King Award seemed to reflect a need to promote the contributions made by
African Americans to the society, arts, and literature. The first book to receive
the Coretta Scott King Award was a biography about the man whose life work
was the impetus for the award. *Dr. Martin Luther King, Jr.: Man of Peace*
was written by Lillie Patterson, school librarian and well-regarded writer of
children's nonfiction.

In 1971, the winner was *Black Troubadour: Langston Hughes* written
by Charlemae Rollins. In addition to granting the Coretta Scott King
Award to this literary biography of the esteemed poet, the committee
selected eight honor books, including several that were originally published for adult readers but thought to have appeal for young people, such
as Maya Angelou's *I Know Why the Caged Bird Sings*. This undoubtedly
reflected the limited number of books written by African American writers for children.

The Committee bestowed its first illustrator award to George Ford for his
drawings in *Ray Charles*, by Sharon Bell Mathis, who won the author award
for the lively text in 1974. This selection was the first of many Coretta Scott
King Awards that celebrated black music.

Occasionally, a person whose prominence was outside the field produced
work the Committee deemed worthy of note. For example, Pearl Bailey, the
legendary entertainer, was a winner for her book *Duey's Tale* and celebrated

actor and playwright, Ossie Davis was the 1979 winner for *Escape to Freedom: A Play about Young Frederick Douglass*.

While many of the books highlighted during this period were inspirational biographies, one notable novel that received an author honor recognition was Mildred Taylor's *Roll of Thunder, Hear My Cry*. This trailblazing work was also awarded the John Newbery Medal, the highest accolade given in children's literature and only the second awarded to an African American writer since this esteemed recognition began in 1922.

THE 1980s

The decade began with recognition for Walter Dean Myers's *The Young Landlords*. Mr. Myers then went on to become the writer who has received the largest number of awards from the various Coretta Scott King Committees. This highly skilled and prolific writer has won nearly every accolade available in the field and he continued to create interesting and thought provoking work for children and teen readers in a variety of genres until his death in 2014.

In addition, this period saw a number of interesting developments in the field of African American children's books because writers who had established themselves in the adult market were compelled to write for younger readers. Alice Childress and Julius Lester, who were established adult authors, were recipients of author honors during this time.

This decade was also a period of multiple recognitions for a writer who made an indelible mark on all children's publishing: Virginia Hamilton. Hamilton, the first African American to win a John Newbery Medal, received seven author awards and honor recognitions during the Eighties. The list of books was as varied as it was distinguished: there were realistic novels, retellings of fairy tales, works of fantasy, and historical biographies. Before her death in 2002, Virginia Hamilton became the first children's writer awarded a MacArthur Foundation "Genius" award.

During the 1980s, The Coretta Scott King Committee recognized innovators and (re)introduced the work of prolific illustrators. First, the Committee expanded its definition of illustrations by awarding the Coretta Scott King Award for Illustration to Peter Mugabane for his book of photographs *Black Child*. Its haunting images of South African children made the connection to the African Diaspora for young readers.

This time period celebrated one of the premier picture book artists: Jerry Pinkney. With a focused attention to detail, Pinkney's lively watercolor paintings brought richness to every story he illustrated. His work in *Mirandy and Brother Wind* and *The Patchwork Quilt* defined African American picture books.

The Coretta Scott King Award organization established a new award in order to support debut artists. The John Steptoe Award for New Talent pays homage to his legacy each year given to promising writers and illustrators. This recognition is in honor of Steptoe's lushly illustrated retelling of the Cinderella story *Mufaro's Beautiful Daughters*, which presented a more positive view of Africa while retelling the Cinderella story. Steptoe, one of the youngest illustrators in the field, passed away in 1989. His talent and style cannot be underestimated. His major impact on the stylistic vision of books about young people of color continues on today thirty years after his passing.

In addition, special citation was given to Coretta Scott King in 1984. Her compilation of *The Words of Martin Luther King, Jr.* remains a necessary reminder of the contributions of this legendary civil rights leader. In one volume, a reader can find quotations, speeches, sermons, and other selected writings. Specifically included are his two most famous speeches: "I Have a Dream" (August 28, 1963) and "I've Been the Mountaintop" (April 3, 1968).

THE 1990s

By the 1990s, the Coretta Scott King Award Committee looked exclusively at books from children's publishing. While there were still a small number of books produced by African American writers and illustrators within the adult market, the Committee no longer had to look there to round out its list. This decade saw a profusion of well-researched and lively written fiction and nonfiction works.

A Long Hard Journey: The Story of the Pullman Porter by Patricia C. and Frederick L. McKissack provides insight into the struggle for equality that preceded the Civil Rights Movement; and Walter Dean Myers wove his family story into his compelling narrative in *Now Is Your Time: The African American Struggle for Freedom*. These novels demonstrated a high level of sophistication in the storytelling and literary aspects.

Angela Johnson received her first Coretta Scott King author award for *Toning the Sweep*, a poetic multigenerational story of loss and reconciliation. She would go on to receive awards for another novel and a collection of poetry. Sharon Draper would begin her tenure as a multiple winner with *Forged by Fire*, a hard-hitting novel about a young man struggling with the gritty side of urban life.

Rita Williams-Garcia used her considerable talent to uncover the humanity of a streetwise teen mother in *Like Sisters on the Homefront*. Two unique story collections—*Dark Thirty: Southern Tales of the Supernatural* by Patricia A. McKissack and *Her Stories* by Virginia Hamilton—were spotlighted. Both volumes are rooted in the African American tradition of storytelling. *Dark*

Thirty: Southern Tales of the Supernatural weaves black history throughout its stories of mystery and magic, while *Her Stories* focuses on the odd and eerie in the lives of its female subjects.

The illustrator awards during this period celebrated established artists who continued their excellent work and new artists who brought new energy to the field. Leo and Diane Dillon's *Aida*, a well-known tale of the Ethiopian princess-turned-slave, her soldier lover, and their inevitable tragedy, acknowledged their fresh and unique portrayal of this tale. Their work brought new audiences to this story, and their style became recognizable and assumed its steadfast place in the canon of illustrators of literature for young people.

The story quilt art of Faith Ringgold was welcomed into children's books with *Tar Beach*, a story that did not shy away from harsh economic realities even as it celebrated the bond of family. Similar in theme but with strong oil paintings, totally different in style was *Uncle Jed's Barbershop*, illustrated by James Ransome. Further, the illustrators interpreted difficult issues of African American life in a picture book format. Through this manner they made visible the hard realities of economic uncertainty and racial injustice.

Another generation in the Pinkney clan came to the forefront as Brian Pinkney deployed his unique scratchboard technique to enliven *Sukey and the Mermaid* and *The Faithful Friend*, stories from the folk culture of South Carolina and the Caribbean. Another of the new generation was Javaka Steptoe, who continued his father's tradition of award-winning art with various artistic styles in *In Daddy's Arms I am Tall: African Americans Celebrating Fathers*.

The eagerly anticipated and visually stunning *The Middle Passage: White Ships Black Cargo* by Tom Feelings demonstrated power of images to move viewers as much as a compelling narrative. Feelings used few words and arresting black and white drawings to tell the devastating story of the enslaved Africans who built America.

2000–2009

The first Coretta Scott King Award winner of the new century was historic. For the first time, one book won both the Coretta Scott King Award and the John Newbery Medal. Christopher Paul Curtis became the first African American male to win the Newbery for his stunning novel *Bud, Not Buddy*. This story of an orphan seeking his father in Michigan during the Great Depression continues to be one of the most popular award winners in children's literature.

Other trailblazing books were created by prominent African American writers. *Monster*, by Walter Dean Myers, departed from traditional narrative in order to experiment with format. He used screenplay format, as written by the main character, to engage teen readers and received an honor recognition. It also had the distinction of winning the first the Michael L. Printz Award for Excellence in Young Adult Literature (2019) for literary achievement in a YA novel.

Novels for teen readers distinguished themselves with books exploring the family unit within contemporary realistic fiction or historical fiction. *Miracle's Boys*, Woodson's novel of three brothers struggling to remain a family in the face of tremendous loss, demonstrates her mastery of spare lyrical prose. Two accomplished yet very different depictions of slavery were explored in Draper's *Copper Sun* and Curtis's *Elijah of Buxton*. Nobel Laureate Toni Morrison's essay accompanying photographs of the Civil Rights era was heralded by the Committee and brought her powerful language to younger readers.

The power of poetry to connect with young readers was on full display during this period. Grimes's novel in verse, *Bronx Masquerade*, provides an emotional bond with its cast of high school character. Nelson, an established poet, brought her talents to the field and received honor recognition for three collections: *Carver: A Life in Poems*; *Fortune's Bones: The Manumission Requiem*; and *A Wreath for Emmett Till*. Nelson used challenging poetic forms to illuminate African American history. Poetry about the life of jazz great Billie Holiday by Weatherford was also recognized.

As in previous periods, this decade saw the rise of immense artistic talent in the illustrator category. Collier's brilliant use of collage technique earned him the illustrator award for his debut picture book *Uptown*. His fresh interpretation of Giovanni's text for *Rosa* made a familiar story compelling. Watercolorist E. B. Lewis brought poignancy and power to his depiction of aviator Bessie Coleman in *Talkin' about Bessie: The Story of Aviator Elizabeth Coleman*.

Christie utilized an expressionistic style to honor awardees *Only Passing Through: The Story of Sojourner Truth* and *Brothers in Hope*. Christopher Myers followed his father Walter Dean Myers into the field, as an illustrator rather than writer. His paintings in *Black Cat* and *Jazz* were bold and atmospheric. The traditional literature genre was well represented as Ashley Bryan received acclaim for two of his works that employed his vivid use of color, *Beautiful Blackbird* and *Let It Shine*.

There is no doubt, however, that the illustrator of the decade is Kadir Nelson. Nelson's dramatic illustrations in *Ellington Was Not a Street* and *Moses: When Harriet Tubman Led Her People to Freedom* were arresting and earned illustrator awards. Ironically, it was Nelson's writing in *We Are the Ship: The Story of Negro League Baseball* that garnered the Coretta Scott King author award in 2009. His bold illustrations did not go unrecognized by the Committee: they received an honor recognition.

In 2009, winner for illustration was Floyd Cooper for his warm illustrations in *The Blacker the Berry*, a collection of Joyce Carol Thomas's poems that celebrate the beauty to be found in the range of skin tone colors of African American children. Her poems were recognized as an honor recipient. Other honor recognitions for writing included poetic works by Hope Anita Smith, for *Keeping the Night Watch* and a biography in verse *Becoming Billie Holiday* by Carole Boston Weatherford.

Jerry Pinkney added to his large number of Coretta Scott King illustrator honors with *The Moon over Star* and Sean Qualls for *Before John Was a Jazz Giant*. The John Steptoe Award for New Talent put a much deserved spotlight on Shadra Strickland for her poignant drawings in *Bird*. These celebrated books served as an excellent gateway into the next decade of the Coretta Scott King Award.

2010–2018

The Coretta Scott King Book Awards has excelled at bringing unknown stories to the forefront on children's literature. The 2010 award winner *Bad News for Outlaws: The Remarkable Life of Bass Reeves, Deputy U.S. Marshal*, written by Vaunda Micheaux Nelson and illustrated by R. Gregory Christie, featured an African American lawman from the American West. The illustrator award featured photographs accompanying an iconic poem. Charles R. Smith, Jr., illustrator of *My People*, text by Langston Hughes brought luminous images and served to connect the text to a contemporary audience.

Honors went to Tanith Davis for her YA novel *Mare's War*, which is about modern teens discovering their grandmother's role in World War II, and illustrator E. B. Lewis's lush watercolors in *The Negro Speaks of Rivers* enhanced another Langston Hughes's iconic poem. The John Steptoe Award for New Talent introduced Kekla Magoon, author of *The Rock and the River*, a novel that explores how the tension between two different philosophies for seeking racial justice impacts one family.

This year also saw the first Coretta Scott King-Virginia Hamilton Award for Lifetime Achievement.

The Coretta Scott King-Virginia Hamilton Award for Lifetime Achievement is named in memory of beloved children's author Virginia Hamilton. The annual award is presented in even years to an African American author, illustrator or author/illustrator for a body of his or her published books for children and/ or young adults, and who has made a significant and lasting literary contribution. The recipient of the inaugural award was Walter Dean Myers in 2010. In odd years, the award is presented to a practitioner for substantial contributions through active engagement with youth using award winning African American literature for children and/or young adults, via implementation of reading and reading related activities/programs. (American Library Association, 2019b).

Walter Dean Myers, with his influential body of work, was an excellent choice to launch this addition to the Coretta Scott King Awards. The 2010 collection of Award and Honors recipients introduced young readers to unknown heroes, reimagined canonical texts, and amplified a pioneer children's and YA literature through a new award.

In 2011, Rita Williams-Garcia made a successful foray into middle-grade fiction with her author award–winning title, *One Crazy Summer*. Three endearing sisters take a cross-country trip to reunite with their mother who has a connection to the Oakland Black Panther Party. The illustrator award went to Bryan Collier for his collage art in *Dave the Potter: Artist, Poet, Slave*, written by Laban Carrick Hill.

Three very different books received honor recognition. *Lockdown* by Walter Dean Myers takes readers inside the mind of a juvenile facility detainee. The impact of Hurricane Katrina is explored in *Ninth Ward* by Jewell Parker Rhodes. *Yummy: The Last Days of a Southside Shorty*, a graphic novel based on an urban tragedy by G. Neri, showcased the variety of formats used to tell the stories of African Americans; it was selected as an Honor book in 2011.

There was one illustrator honor book: *Jimi: Sounds Like a Rainbow: A Story of the Young Jimi Hendrix* with art by Javaka Steptoe. Two new book creators were recognized with the John Steptoe New Talent Award. The text award went to Victoria Bond and T. R. Simon, authors of *Zora and Me*, for a historical mystery, and illustrator appreciation to Sonia Lynn Sadler, illustrator of *Seeds of Change: Wangari's Gift to the World*, a story of the Kenyan environmentalist and Nobel Prize winner.

The following year, 2012, saw Kadir Nelson again receiving the author award for his writing and an illustrator honor for *Heart and Soul: The Story of America and African Americans*, an ambitious look at the role of blacks in American history, richly enhanced by Nelson's arresting paintings. The illustrator award went to Shane W. Evans, author and illustrator of *Underground: Finding the Light to Freedom*, a work that presents slavery in an age appropriate way for younger readers.

The two author honor books dealt sensitively with difficult topics: *The Great Migration: Journey to the North* by Greenfield, and *Never Forgotten* by McKissack, a novel in verse about a young African kidnapped and sold into slavery. The Lifetime Achievement went to another icon of the field, writer-illustrator Ashley Bryan. Bryan's folklore retellings and signature artwork over decades are a significant contribution to the field. Again, the Coretta Scott King Award Committee amplified books and book creators were unafraid to share the diasporas, both physical and emotional, of African Americans.

Variety among award winners continued to be a theme in 2013. The author award went to Andrea Davis Pinkney for her lively collective biography *Hand in Hand: Ten Black Men Who Changed America*. Many of the subjects in Pinkney's volume are familiar, but her unique voice brought a new understanding for today's readers. Bryan Collier won another illustrator award for *I, Too, Am America* with his multilayered collage artwork of Langston Hughes's famous poem. Like Pinkney's text, Collier's collage art style enlivens a classic poem for contemporary readers.

The books selected for honor books ranged from a quiet yet effective story about bullying, Jacqueline Woodson's *Each Kindness* to a novel with an unusual format, *No Crystal Stair: A Documentary Novel of the Life and Work of Lewis Micheaux, Harlem Bookseller*, written by Vaunda Micheaux Nelson.

The illustrator honors recognized the work of one newcomer and two previous winners. Daniel Minter's block print illustrations enlivened *Ellen's Broom* as the story depicts the era immediately following slavery. The vibrant colors and lively art in Christopher Myers's *H. O. R. S. E.: A Game of Basketball and Imagination* reflects the energy of urban sports culture. Kadir Nelson added another illustrator honor with his bold portrait-like illustrations paired with Dr. Martin Luther King, Jr.'s most famous speech in "I Have a Dream."

Rita Williams-Garcia demonstrated her deft touch at blending themes of family, coming of age, and social issues with the 2014 author award–winning *P. S. Be Eleven*, the sequel to *One Crazy Summer*. Bryan Collier's illustrator award for *Knock Knock: My Dad's Dream for Me* also featured an urban landscape through his accomplished collage images.

Three honor books presented different aspects of African American history. Congressman John Lewis and Andrew Aydin provided the text for a graphic depiction of Lewis's experiences in the Civil Rights Movement in *March: Book One*. The much decorated Walter Dean Myers's *Darius and Twig* uses the friendship between two young men to explore two paths to a better life and Nikki Grimes celebrates the special relationship between a teacher and a troubled student in *Words with Wings*. An illustrator honor went to Kadir Nelson as his powerful art celebrating the life of *Nelson Mandela*.

Patricia and Frederick McKissack were awarded the Coretta Scott King-Virginia Hamilton Award for Lifetime Achievement. This husband and wife team was a multiple Coretta Scott King Award recipient, primarily for their well-researched and student-friendly presentations of informational books about a myriad of topics in African American history.

The 2015 author award went to one of the most decorated books in children's literature, *Brown Girl Dreaming*, by Jacqueline Woodson. This memoir-in-verse with its lyrical language and strong voice set the tone for a year that was rich in poetry offerings. The illustrator honor also reflected a high artistic achievement. Christopher Myers's *Firebird* presents colorful and as fluid images in Misty Copeland's journey to become a ballerina.

Two of the three author honors recipients were also works that used the heightened language of poetry. *The Crossover* by Kwame Alexander employed multiple poetic forms to tell his story of basketball loving twins facing change in their lives. Marilyn Nelson, a former poet laureate of Connecticut, explored her childhood path that led to writing career in *How I Discovered Poetry*. Kekla Magoon's *How It Went Down* tells the story of a tragic shooting through multiple perspectives.

The two illustrator honors focused on books depicting trailblazing female performers. Christian Robinson's energetic artistic style added to *Josephine: The Dazzling Life of Josephine Baker*, while Frank Morrison's elongated paintings supported *Little Melba and Her Big Trombone*. The John Steptoe Award brought to the forefront a fresh new voice in Jason Reynolds in his debut novel, *When I Was the Greatest*.

Coretta Scott King Awards reach a significant milestone 2016. First, history was made when Rita Williams-Garcia became the first to win author awards for three books in a series since Mildred Taylor accomplished that feat. *Gone Crazy in Alabama* saw the conclusion of the stories of the Gaither sisters told with humor and poignancy. The illustrator winner celebrated the unique music and culture of New Orleans native *Trombone Shorty* with colorful spreads by Bryan Collier.

There was a rare occurrence when one writer received honor recognition for two different books. Jason Reynolds was lauded for both *The Boy in the Black Suit* and his collaboration with Brendan Kiely, *All-American Boys*. A third author honor went to a novel based on the life of Malcolm X entitled *X: A Novel*, written by his daughter Ilyasah Shabazz with Kekla Magoon.

Two former recipients were awarded illustrator honors: R. Gregory Christie for his impressionistic paintings in *The Book Itch: Freedom, Truth & Harlem's Greatest Bookstore* and Christian Robinson's evocative art in *Last Stop on Market Street*. There were two John Steptoe awards given. Author Ronald L. Smith was recognized for his gothic middle-grade novel, *Hoodoo*.

Ekua Holmes's highly textured artwork enhanced the bold text of *Voice of Freedom: Fannie Lou Hamer, Spirit of the Civil Rights Movement*. The Coretta Scott King-Virginia Hamilton Award for Lifetime Achievement was awarded to an important figure in children's literature, Jerry Pinkney. Mr. Pinkney's body of work began in the early years of the award, and he continues to produce high-quality work for young readers.

The 2017 author award for *March Book: Three*, the final volume in the trilogy by Congressman John Lewis and Andrew Aydin, demonstrated the power of storytelling in conveying an important aspect of African American history. Nineteen years after winning his first Coretta Scott King illustrator award, Javaka Steptoe was awarded another. This time, he won for his groundbreaking visuals in *Radiant Child: The Story of Young Artist Jean-Michel Basquiat.*

Author awards celebrated a warm family story, *As Brave as You* by Jason Reynolds and the sobering imagined lives of the enslaved in *Freedom over Me: Eleven Slaves, Their Lives and Dreams Brought to Life* by Ashley Bryan. Bryan also received an illustrator honor for the work. The other two illustrator honors were Jerry Pinkney's lush watercolor paintings for *In Plain Sight* and R. Gregory Christie's evocative paintings for *Freedom in Congo Square*. The John Steptoe Award for New Talent for *The Moon Is also a Star* by rising star Nicola Yoon is a timeless story about love and immigration.

The 2018 awards embodied all of the advocacy and quest for excellence that were part of the awards. The author award for *Piecing Me Together* by Renee Watson addressed questions of identity, self-esteem, and desire for success. The illustrator award showcased the versatility of the artistic vision of Ekua Homes in *Out of Wonder: Poems Celebrating Poets*.

Two of the three author honors were searing stories about urban violence and its impact on young people. Jason Reynolds chose the taut language of poetry in *Long Way Down*, while debut author Angie Thomas opted for a multilayered novel in *The Hate You Give*. Derrick Barnes's *Crown: An Ode to the Fresh Cut*, a testament to African American culture as it is reveled in the local barbershop, celebrated both the author award and the illustrator award for Gordon C. James.

The second illustrator honor was awarded to James Ransome for his expressive art in *Before She Was Harriet: The Story of Harriet Tubman*. The John Steptoe Award was awarded to illustrator Charley Palmer for the vibrant art in *Mama Africa! How Miriam Makeba Spread Hope with Her Song*. Eloise Greenfield, a stalwart writer in children's books, was awarded the Coretta Scott King-Virginia Hamilton Award for Lifetime Achievement. Ms. Greenfield's body of work encompassed prose, poetry, fiction, and nonfiction over decades and is still widely read and taught.

CONCLUSION

The Coretta Scott King Book Awards has a full and rich tradition of recognizing the best literature for young people created by African American writers and illustrators. The honored books are of the highest literary and artistic quality and share the universal themes that celebrate the humanity of all. Educators may use resources developed by the Coretta Scott King Award. One of the unique aspects of the Coretta Scott King Book Awards Jury is, in addition to selecting the award-winning titles, the jury is also responsible for preparing book discussion guides.

A number of these guides are available at the Coretta Scott King Book Awards website (American Library Association, 2019a). That same page also offers another tool for educators: TeachingBooks.net CSK Curricular Resource Center (2019). On the journey of nearly fifty years of history, the awards have also introduced, promoted, and encouraged some of the most remarkable creative talent in the field of children's publishing.

REFERENCES

American Library Association. (2019a). Coretta Scott King book awards educational resources. Retrieved from http://www.ala.org/rt/emiert/coretta-scott-king-book-awards-educational-resources.

American Library Association. (2019b). Virginia Hamilton Award for Lifetime Achievement. Retrieved from http://www.ala.org/rt/emiert/virginia-hamilton-award-lifetime-achievement

The TeachingBooks.Net Blog. (2019). Teaching with the CSK Book Award Curriculum Resource Center. Retrieved from https://forum.teachingbooks.net/2009/10/nicks-picks-the-coretta-scott-king-book-award-curriculum-resource-center/

Young Adult Library Services Association. (2019). The Michael L. Printz Award for excellence in young adult literature. Retrieved from http://www.ala.org/yalsa/printz

ADDITIONAL RESOURCES FOR USING CORETTA SCOTT KING BOOKS

Ford, A. (2019). 50 years of the Coretta Scott King book awards. Retrieved from https://americanlibrariesmagazine.org/2019/06/03/50-years-of-csk-book-awards/?fbclid=IwAR10VOwtZ7_1R8f194zwiAdoIidL4zFhgDEIN1Vpg9zjISSb0NmecL ufjjY

McCollough, C. J., & Phelps, A. P. (2014). *The Coretta Scott King Book Awards, 1970–2014* (5th ed.).Chicago, IL: ALA Editions.

Phelps, A. P., McCollough, C. J., & Pavonetti, L. M. (2014). *Coretta Scott King Award books discussion guide: Pathways to democracy.* Chicago, IL: ALA Editions.

Sutton, R. (Ed.) 2019. The CSK Book Awards at 50 [Special issue]. *The Horn Book Magazine*, May/June.

Chapter 2

Themes and Critical Foundation of Early African American Authors of Young Adult Literature

Shanetia P. Clark

Marian Wright Edelman, the Founder and President of the Children's Defense Fund, wrote in her piece "It's Hard to Be What You Can't See" (2015) about the power of stories:

> When we think about what it is to be "connected," we think about memory. We think about history. We think about storytelling. All of these words that we hear—"literacy," "inclusion," "diversity"—those are all words for connection. . . . When I say to people "why do we need to have diverse books?" it's not because necessarily everybody needs to see themselves reflected in every book, but because we need that sense of connection. We need to live in a global sense.

This sense of connection—common experiences, language, and culture, vis-a-vis the written word, motivated the forefathers and foremothers of African American YA literature. Their stories served as the vehicle through which young people—especially African American—could find communion with one another. YA literature that told robust stories of African American youth held the space for its readers to be seen and edified in ways that had been missing previously.

Scholar Dr. Rudine Sims Bishop built upon the seminal study by Larrick (1965) of the "all white world of children's literature." She further exposed "the children's book world for failing to include African Americans in children's books, but also for feeding White children 'gentle doses of racism' through their books" (Edelman, 2015, para. 4). Such destructive trends were advanced by the lack of and access to stories that placed African Americans in positive and realistic light. The foundation laid by the authors presented in this volume sought to disrupt these trends by showcasing and illuminating more robust portraits of African Americans.

In her 1980 study, Bishop examined a collection of texts that centered around African Americans. She noted three distinct categories in the books. First were "social conscience" books, ones that "with a few exceptions, the primary audience for those books is White readers who are being encouraged to develop a social conscience—an awareness of social injustice and of their responsibility to help make things right" (Bishop, 2012). Next she examined the manner "to which a distinctive African American cultural experience was reflected in the books" (Bishop, 2012, p. 6). Finally, the third category identified "culturally conscious" books; these

> set out to reflect both the distinctiveness of African American cultural experiences and the universality of human experience. These books are set in Black cultural environments, have Black major characters, are told from the perspective of those characters, and include some textual means of identifying the characters as Black, such as physical descriptions or distinctive cultural markers. (Bishop, 2012, p. 7)

The three distinctive categories are critical. The authors and the work discussed in this collection are one that Rudine Sims-Bishop described as "'culturally conscious' [because] they recognize the genuine experiences and subtleties of African-American life" (Brooks, 2006, p. 375).

Contemporary authors like award-winning author Jason Reynolds explained why his books center around black characters. He responded, "Because it's okay for Black kids to be in Black space, uninterrupted sometimes" (personal communication, Reynolds, April 24, 2019). Young people can have their own stories within their own spaces where their humanity, their joys, fears, laughters, and loves—their validity and divinity—are at the forefront.

YA literature, like children's literature, provides a space and a haven for young people to see their lives as unique and special. Reynolds celebrates and acknowledges the path set forth the profound impact of the scholarship of Bishop and the Coretta Scott King Award and as well as the techniques, craft, and stories by the African American YA literature authors presented in this volume.

These African American authors and scholars held the space for the stories of African American youth. They wrote stories that were centered around African American experiences, families, and lives. In this volume, the authors presented the historical context and recognition that the trailblazing African American authors broadened the landscape of YA literature. They expanded the access of African American stories for adolescents and their experiences. They shined a light on the facets of the dynamic culture, challenges, and celebrations in the African American community through stories that were geared toward adolescents.

Collins recognized the potential effect of literature that centers African American characters and its profound effects; she explains, "This literature can provide black young adults with a means of transcending racism and segregation, can lead them to self–discovery, and can help them eliminate whatever sense of isolation or alienation they may have. It can also help them overcome entrenched personal problems" (Collins, 1993). Collin's assertions still ring true. However, for YA literature to serve as a vehicle through which transformation can occur, black youth must have access to high-quality texts. The power of the literature rests with the readers.

Dr. Ebony Elizabeth Thomas agrees with this assertion, and goes a step further. She asserts that an "imagination gap [is present and] is caused in part by the lack of diversity in childhood and teen life depicted in children's books and media" (Thomas, 2016, p. 112). An imagination gap limits adolescents' view of the world. This gap contributes to a narrow view of African American youth, and that, as evidenced by Bishop and other scholars' work (Harris, 1999, 2009, 2011; Tatum, 2006), is destructive because it still exists.

The movement, initiated by Virginia Hamilton, Walter Dean Myers, Mildred Taylor, Julius Lester, and the like, who served as the impetus to publish and present a richer tapestry of books that depict African American life, remains critical to enriching the tapestry of literature for young people. The imagination gap may be lessened or expanded by librarians, teachers, and teacher educators, for they, oftentimes, are the ones who connect young people to books.

Connections to books that center around the African Americans and their experiences provide a unique lens and framework from which African American adolescents can critique and commune in the world. The authors in this text have provided the books, and now the critics and scholars are not only advocating for these books but also beginning to seriously analyze their foundational influence in terms of themes and ideological stances.

Scholar Wanda Brooks conducted a study with an 8th-grade reading class at a northeastern urban public school in Pennsylvania. Of the class of twenty-eight, one "self-identified" as Puerto Rican, one as Dominican/African American, and the rest as African American. Her study focused on young people reading and reflecting on "culturally conscious" books (Brooks, 2006, p. 378). She highlighted that the participants' responses to the texts could be categorized as the following—recurring themes, linguistic patterns, and ethnic group practices.

Within these larger categories, these young readers highlighted themes of forging family and friend relationships, confronting and overcoming racism, surviving city life, African American Vernacular English, and beliefs in the supernatural (Brooks, 2006, pp. 383–384). These young readers sought for aspects of their lives to be reflected in the books by Virginia Hamilton and Walter Dean Myers, whose work requires readers to demonstrate reading flexibility.

Brooks's study advances the consideration that teachers and teacher educators must have when bringing and introducing texts to adolescent readers. She reminds readers, "As the data indicated, however, interpretations and uses of culture while reading can never be taken for granted or presumed similar, even across individuals from similar racial or ethnic backgrounds" (Brooks, 2006, p. 390). The 8th-grade readers in her study demonstrated to Brooks—as well as to teachers and teacher educators—that racial and ethnic commonalities among the stories' characters and the authors are important, but they cannot be the sole entry point into a text.

Other aspects to the story should be shared, such as important aspects of adolescent lives such as peer relationships, family relationships, and the developments of the sense of self. Disrupting the perception of a singular, universal reading of African American YA literature arises within the study. Hence, the call for greater variety of points of view, formats, and genres that explore African American young adults is tremendously important.

Even if the readers and the authors and illustrators have the same racial and cultural backgrounds, young readers can still have a "disavowal and negative responses [that] need to be read and analyzed within their specific racial and cultural context" (Gardner, 2017, p. 122).

Gardner, who was discussing young people's responses to picturebooks specially, posits that the "children's response [to visual images] raises critical questions about the ways in which racial identities and visuality intersect, and how social structures like race can influence and confound children's interpretive responses" (Gardner, 2017, p. 122). To hypothesize their response even further, the same discussions and insights would be evident in YA literature written by African Americans.

The African American authors of YA literature assume an awesome responsibility to unpack and explore, either explicitly or implicitly, the manner in which African Americans adolescents navigate through and within society. Brooks, among other scholars, implores teachers and teacher educators: "African American literature, as well as all multicultural books, contains various entry points [i.e., using textual features] for students from all ethnicities.

Unless we analyze books for these entry points, teachers may be limited by how they use these books pedagogically" (Brooks, 2006, p. 390). As teachers and teacher educators supporting young people navigate their world, the powerful possibilities of YA literature cannot be understated.

Texts have to potential to reaffirm, modify, or refute a reader's concept of the world (Collins, 1993, para. 15). This assertion remains the foundation through which teachers and teacher educators help to facilitate conversations with young people. Yet before conversations and (re)examinations of particular texts' connections, young people must gain access to these texts. Teacher and teacher educators are often viewed as gatekeepers to books by providing entry points to the students.

Likewise, scholar Violet J. Harris asserts that young people's "[racialized] or gendered responses to texts can excite and frighten. Excitement can stem from the inclusion of new intellectual perspective and voices, radical structures or formats, or the sense that a work symbolizes a major cultural shift" (1999). Young people who gain access to texts that affirm their lived experiences and voices find both an aesthetic and efferent reading response.

As access remains at the forefront, the themes and critical foundations that teachers and teacher educators should elicit in today's middle and high schools and undergraduate methods courses can only be enacted if students can read the books. The four authors covered here produced works of art. Educators do consider their texts as works of art, but are these works available? Are the works of the African American authors following in their footsteps accessible as well? The access and analysis of art remains important.

Mary Stone Hanley states, when considering the redistribution of arts (i.e., access to texts), that art is a "resource for human sense-making, communication, and adaptation; they have been a way to record history, shape culture, and promote imagination, conceptualization, and individual and social transformation. They are multiple symbol systems in a world of symbolic meaning-making. Access to the arts and artmaking is essential to a comprehensive education for all young people."

The question remains, How do we, as teachers and teacher educators, support our students' exploration and critical analysis of YA literature, in particular those written by the African American forefathers and foremothers? Do these texts enable African American youth to see themselves? Do they find greater connections to themselves, school, and the larger community?

At her current university, when Dr. Clark engages her preservice teachers in conversations about how books and classroom libraries are not neutral spaces; therefore, it is imperative that students learned to see whose stories are ignored, what stereotypes are projected, and who is included or excluded. Together they work to illuminate and to disrupt the stereotypes of gender, race, social class, religion, and abilities.

There is an urgency in the field of YA literature. The following are lessons that extend the themes highlighted in this chapter. They could be facilitated with a whole class, a small group, or an individual.

INSTRUCTIONAL ACTIVITIES

A lesson that teacher educators could do with their preservice teachers is an extension of an examination of an individual classroom library. This lesson seeks to explore the common study novels that are selected at the middle school and high school levels. As a whole class, have preservice teachers examine the common study novels that are required for the school or for the district.

The following are some guiding questions to begin the analysis: Whose stories are told? Who are the authors? Are there books written by African American authors? Are there common study novels that tell the stories of African American youth? If contemporary realistic fiction or historical fiction, do these stories represent, articulate, and/or celebrate the African American youth experience during this time period? What reoccuring themes arise throughout these common study novels? Do these common study novels reflect the demographics of the district? If not, consider why books, similar to ones highlighted in this collection, are, or are not, included.

This lesson is aligned with the IRA/NCTE Standards 1, 2, and 7 of the English Language Arts:

1. **Standard 1**: Students read a wide range of print and nonprint texts to build an understanding of texts, of themselves, and of the cultures of the United States and the world; to acquire new information; to respond to the needs and demands of society and the workplace; and for personal fulfillment. Among these texts are fiction and nonfiction, classic and contemporary works.
2. **Standard 2**: Students read a wide range of literature from many periods in many genres to build an understanding of the many dimensions (e.g., philosophical, ethical, and aesthetic) of human experience.
3. **Standard 7**: Students conduct research on issues and interests by generating ideas and questions, and by posing problems. They gather, evaluate, and synthesize data from a variety of sources (e.g., print and nonprint texts, artifacts, and people) to communicate their discoveries in ways that suit their purpose and audience.

For a small-group exercise, invite students to identify with a character within a novel written by an African American author, in particular one who is showcased in this collection. Have the students utilize the Uta Hagen framework to unpack the motivations, obstacles, and actions of a particular character. To engage preservice teachers' background knowledge and thinking, show the video of Uta Hagen guiding her acting students in the Working Arts Library Master Class to examine how clothing dictated characters' movements and perceptions of social etiquette in a play set the Victorian Era.

She challenged her acting students to reach beyond the crisis (the conflict) of the central character and imagine how the sources, including the fashion, influence and shape the character.

Take a character that you may be going to work on or that you always wanted to work on . . . [Take] him or her out of the crisis in which they find themselves in the given play and give them a simple task that's something they might do every day or that they something . . . I did yesterday or I'm going to do after the crisis is over so that I start to discover all the sources that make it different than it is now and to see if I can put my character into a time and place so that I believe I lived there. (June 27, 2009)

Use this expanded view of a character to respond and reflect on the Uta Hagen's nine questions that actors use unpack a character they are portraying. These questions include the following: (1) Who am I? [See a video of unpacking this question (Acting Truth, 2015).] (2) What time is it? (3) Where am I? (4) What surrounds me? (5) What are my given circumstances? (6) What are my relationships? (7) What do I want? (8) What is in my way? and (9) What do I do to get what I want? Creating a character sketch is aligned with Standard 3 of the IRA/NCTE Standards for the English Language Arts:

Students apply a wide range of strategies to comprehend, interpret, evaluate, and appreciate texts. They draw on their prior experience, their interactions with other readers and writers, their knowledge of word meaning and of other texts, their word identification strategies, and their understanding of textual features (e.g., sound-letter correspondence, sentence structure, context, graphics).

These questions enable actors (readers) to slow down. These questions are grounded in the text. Text-dependent questions are fundamental supporting actors, preservice teachers, and readers to anchor their reading in the text and move toward themes and ideas that reach beyond the four corners of the work. Creating a character sketch is aligned with Standard 3:

Students apply a wide range of strategies to comprehend, interpret, evaluate, and appreciate texts. They draw on their prior experience, their interactions with other readers and writers, their knowledge of word meaning and of other texts, their word identification strategies, and their understanding of textual features (e.g., sound-letter correspondence, sentence structure, context, graphics).

At the Spring 2019 "Diverse Voices in Latinx Children's Literature" at the Bank Street Center for Children's Literature, Rudy Gutierre, a panelist, made a comment about his guiding inspiration for his work. He shared how "his life experiences [served] as research for his books and how his mom didn't know/ see her validity and divinity" (ProfesoraEspana, 2019), this motivation for him to illustrate these stories. He noted the power of books for young people. He said that enables them to see both their validity and divinity.

Therefore, for the individual student exercise, teacher educators can have their preservice teachers create and perform a monologue from a character's point of view. This monologue is an extension of the small-group lesson that call for the analysis of a character. The essential question of "Why?" guides the strategic writing process (Dean, 2017). Moreover, this monologue will enable to make public the voice, motivations, and actions of a character; in other words, it will illuminate the validity and divinity of the character.

This lesson is aligned with Standard 4 (Students adjust their use of spoken, written, and visual language—for example, conventions, style, and vocabulary— to communicate effectively with a variety of audiences and for different purposes) of the IRA/NCTE Standards for the English Language Arts.

CONCLUSION

The themes and critical foundations of the pillars of African American YA literature center around identity and agency. The forefathers and foremothers of YA literature, the ones discussed in this book, sought to make visible the humanity and culture of African American youth, across a variety of time periods and places.

To invite a critical reading of literature for young people, educators must acknowledge the importance of gaining access to texts written by African American authors and illustrators (and other creators of color), refute stereotypes, move beyond essentialism, and bring forth the historical context, assimilations, resistance, and transactions as they are manifested in physical and cultural characteristics (Harris, 1999). The literature created by the authors in this collection acknowledges the importance of their voices on behalf of their readers, both young and old.

REFERENCES

Acting Truth. (June 25, 2015). Who am I? (character development)—1 minute acting lesson [YouTube video]. Retrieved from https://www.youtube.com/watch?v=I2pAR11NiIg

Bishop, R. S. (2012). Reflections on the development of African American children's literature. *Journal of Children's Literature*, 38(2), 5–13.

Brooks, W. (2006). Reading representations of themselves: Urban youth use culture and African American textual features to develop literary understandings. *Reading Research Quarterly*, 41(3), 372–392.

Collins, C. J. (1993). A tool for change: Young adult literature in the lives of young adult African–Americans. *Library Trends, 1993*, 378.

Dean, D. (2017). *Strategic writing: The writing process and beyond in the secondary English classroom* (2nd ed.). Urbana, IL: National Council of Teachers of English.

Edelman, M. W. (2015). It's hard to be what you can't see. Retrieved from https://www.childrensdefense.org/child-watch-columns/health/2015/its-hard-to-be-what-you-cant-see/

Harris, V. J. (1999). Applying critical theories to children's literature. *Theory into Practice, 38*(3), 147–154.

Harris, V. J. (2009). We, too, sing America. *The Reading Teacher, 62*(5), 450–455.

Harris, V. J. (2011). Stories from hopescapes. *The Reading Teacher, 64*(5), 380–382.

International Reading Association and the National Council of Teachers of English. (1996). *Standards for the English language arts*. Newark, Delaware: International Reading Association.

Larrick, N. (1965). The all-white world of children's books. *Saturday Review*, Sept. 11, 63–65 & 84–85.

ProfesoraEspana. (2019, March 9). Rudy Gutierrez talking about his life experiences as research for his books and how his mom didn't know/see her validity and divinity, this motivation for him to illustrate these stories. Now I'm crying and how am I to get it together before afternoon panel?! #BSCLatinx2019 [Tweet]. Retrieved from https://twitter.com/ProfesoraEspana/status/1104414184543080448

Tatum, A. W. (2006). Engaging African American males in reading. *Educational Leadership, 63*(5), 44–49.

Thomas, E. E. (2016). Stories *still* matter: Rethinking the role of diverse children's literature today. *Language Arts, 94*(2), 112–119.

The Working Arts. (June 27, 2009). Master class with legendary acting teacher Uta Hagen [YouTube video]. Retrieved from https://www.youtube.com/watch?v=xpzLLv-7_JE&list=PLGSaY6T7nOwaskeczQG2WIVOwHXmjGskF

Part II

FOUNDING AUTHORS AND THEIR EARLY INTRODUCTION

Chapter 3

Walter Dean Myers

A Lifetime of Stories

Ngozi Onuora

CRITICAL RECEPTION

Walter Dean Myers has provided readers with a lifetime of stories. From his debut children's picture book titled *Where Does the Day Go?* (1969), which was a winner of the now inactive Council on Interracial Books for Children Award, to *Juba! A Novel* (2015), published posthumously, Myers's career as a writer for children has spanned more than four decades. During that time, Myers wrote over 100 titles for a range of age groups and from different genres including poetry, folklore, fantasy, science fiction, historical fiction, memoir, nonfiction, and, of course, contemporary realism, of which he is arguably most known.

The novels Myers authored in the 1970s and many of his novels published later take place in urban settings, portray black life in the inner city for youth, and confront issues of social justice (Bishop, 2007). In her book *Free within Ourselves* (2007), noted children's literature expert Rudine Sims Bishop says this of Myers: "One of the things Myers does is to illuminate and celebrate the culturally distinctive aspects of growing up Black in an American urban environment and in so doing captures something of the universality of that experience" (p. 210). This universality and widespread appeal to a variety of readers distinguished Myers's work.

Myers's authentic depictions of adolescent black youth in literature contribute to the illumination of an African American perspective. He also created breakthrough novels such as *Scorpions* (1988), a 1989 Newbery Honor Award winner, dealing with the harsh realities of gang life in Harlem, and novels that introduced innovative storytelling techniques as in *Monster* (1999), the inaugural winner of the Michael Printz Award in 2000 and a *New York Times* Bestseller (McNair, 2010; Lamolinara, 2012, para. 7).

The year 2019 marks the thirtieth anniversary of the publication of *Scorpions*, and current headlines prove that the message and themes of this book are still relevant today. *Scorpions* is coming-of-age story about a twelve-year-old boy named Jamal faced with bullying at school, violent street life in his Harlem neighborhood, and the pull of gangs, as he tries to keep his family unit from fraying.

In the novel *Monster* (1999), Myers used screenplay format, diary, flashback, and other experimental writing techniques to portray Steve Harmon, a black teenager standing trial for a violent crime. The format of the book requires readers to actively engage with the text (evidence) and decide for themselves if they believe Steve to be guilty or innocent. Both *Scorpions* and *Monster* are novels at the upper end of the YA category (grades 9–12) and typify Myers's range of writing skills for this age group as he explores similar themes in these two texts.

Kimberly Parker (2008) used books by Walter Dean Myers for research on the emancipatory reading and literary identities of black boys after participating in book club discussions at their high school. She selected Myers's texts due to his ability "to reposition and recreate the images of African American masculinity for young men . . . because he captures the lives of his readers . . . in an intimate and authentic manner" (p. 113). Parker's participants were able to make personal connections and parallel connections because of their familiarity with Myers's work, discussing similar themes from his other books.

The awards and recognition that Myers garnered during his lengthy writing career demonstrate the critical reception of his work that propelled him as a heavy hitter in the world of YA literature, starting with his first Coretta Scott Author Honor Award Winner in 1976, *Fast Sam, Cool Clyde, and Stuff* (1975). Friendship is a common theme in Myers's YA novels, and this coming-of-age story is about a twelve-year-old boy named Francis who moves into a Harlem neighborhood and meets a group of friends that share an eventful year together.

Fast Sam is geared toward readers in grades 4–7, which encompasses part of the lower end of the YA category (Association of Illinois Middle Grade Schools [AIMS], Mission Statement, n.d.). Because literary canons have historically relegated African American literature for children as invisible (Harris, 1990), Myers's *Fast Sam* exemplified the role children's books could play in portraying young black children in everyday situations, developing meaningful relationships, and navigating life in ordinary and extraordinary ways.

Literacy researchers are also concerned about visibility in literature. Alfred Tatum's research focuses on black adolescent males and reading (Tatum, 2005). Tatum posits that many of the problems black adolescent males face can be linked to the invisibility they feel and that this is a common theme in much of the literature about black males (p. 6). Tatum recollects his teen years and recalls many of the black boys with whom he attended school began to associate with neighborhood gangs. Myers's work acknowledges this existence and the complexity of feelings and decision-making attached with this experience.

As such, Tatum (2005) urges careful selection of materials to get boys, and black boys in particular, involved in reading texts with male characters that address issues they care about, in which they can personally relate, and in whom they can engage emotionally as an avenue toward authentic discussions about masculinity and identity. Tatum's recommendations for "must-read" texts include several by Walter Dean Myers: *Slam!* (1996), *Monster* (1999), *The Greatest* (2000), and *The Beast* (2003).

Tatum also recommends a variety of other texts that feature renowned authors such as James Baldwin, Richard Wright, Ralph Ellison, and Walter Mosley. Placing Myers in the company, these luminary authors speak to the quality of his work and of the importance of YA literature in developing active, lifelong readers. Knowing and understanding the students in your classroom and structuring literacy experiences and instructional strategies around carefully selected literature materials that are relevant to young people's lives exemplify culturally responsive teaching (Gay, 2000).

According to Rudine Sims Bishop (2007), the field of African American YA fiction was "carried by Walter Dean Myers and Virginia Hamilton" in the 1980s, and very few other black authors emerged during that time (p. 221). Prior to *Scorpions*, Myers wrote other gritty urban novels for young adults such as *Hoops* (1981), *Won't Know Till I Get There* (1982), *Motown and Didi* (1984), *The Outside Shot* (1984), *Crystal* (1987), and *Me, Mop, and the Moondance Kid* (1988), not to mention a host of other books from different genres.

Motown and Didi, the 1985 Coretta Scott King Author Winner, is a contemporary love story between two black youth in Harlem dealing with challenges of the 1980s drug scene in urban New York. This book is one of the first YA novels that portrayed an authentic black teen romance. Even today, most YA (and adult) romance depicts romantic relationships between white teens. Thus, having black love represented as contemporary, natural, and authentic, normalizes these experiences for black youth. The paucity of romance novels portraying positive black love not set during chattel slavery is noted (Rosman, 2017).

In addition to major American Library Association (ALA) awards such as Coretta Scott King, Newbery, and Caldecott Awards, Walter Dean Myers has been recognized several times on the lists of ALA Notable Children's Books, and three of his books became National Book Award Finalists (see table 3.1). Myers also earned spots on Top 10 Best Books for Young Adults published by Young Adult Library Services Association (YALSA) in 1997 for a photo

Table 3.1   Book Awards for Walter Dean Myers

Book Award	Book and Year Award Was Won
National Book Award Finalist, Young People's Literature	1999—*Monster* (1999) 2005—*Autobiography of My Dead Brother* (2005) 2010—*Lockdown* (2010)
Coretta Scott King author award	1980—*The Young Landlords* (1979) 1985—*Motown and Didi* (1984) 1989—*Fallen Angels* (1988) 1992—*Now Is Your Time! The African American Struggle for Freedom* (1991) 1997—*Slam!* (1996)
Coretta Scott King Author Honor Award	1976—*Fast Sam, Cool Clyde, and Stuff* (1975) 1993—*Somewhere in the Darkness* (1992) 1994—*Malcolm X: By Any Means Necessary* (1993) 2000—*Monster* (1999) 2011—*Lockdown* (2010) 2014—*Darius & Twig* (2013)
Coretta Scott King Illustrator Honor Award	1998—*Harlem* (1997) by Walter Dean Myers; illustrated by Christopher Myers 2007—*Jazz* (2006) by Walter Dean Myers; illustrated by Christopher Myers
Michael L. Printz Award	2000—*Monster* (1999)
Newbery Honor Award	1989—*Scorpions* (1988) 1993—*Somewhere in the Darkness* (1992)
Caldecott Honor Award	1998—*Harlem* (1997) by Walter Dean Myers; illustrated by Christopher Myers

essay of African American achievements and experience titled *One More River to Cross* (1996), 1998, for a collaboration with his son on an illustrated poem titled *Harlem* (1997), and 2000 for his highly lauded work, *Monster* (1999) (http://www.ala.org/yalsa/booklists/bbya).

The legacy of Walter Dean Myers is evident in his receipt of the 2010 Coretta Scott King-Virginia Hamilton Award for Lifetime Achievement. The year 2010 was the first year for such an award, and it has been awarded annually ever since. During even-numbered years, the award is granted to an author or illustrator whose body of work represents a "significant and lasting literary contribution" (http://www.ala.org/awardsgrants/awards/339/select).

For odd-numbered years, the award is presented to a "practitioner for substantial contributions through active engagement with youth using award winning African American literature for children and/or young adults, via implementation of reading and reading related activities/programs" (see chapter 1: CSK Award).

The criteria for African American authors or illustrators to receive the Virginia Hamilton Award for Lifetime Achievement are that their body of work has spanned pre-K–grade 12, their writing or illustrations have distinguished them as eminent creators in their field, their published work is recognized as significant and has made a lasting contribution to children's/YA literature by and about African Americans as evidenced by the quality, quantity (at least seven books), and longevity (at least ten years of work in existence) (http://www.ala.org/rt/emiert/virginia-hamilton-award-lifetime-achievement).

On January 18, 2010, the press release announcing Myers as the recipient of this award was made available on the ALA website. Morales and Petersen (2010 January 18) quoted committee chair, Barbara Jones Clark, as saying, "Myers' body of work offers a mirror, validating lives of young people whose varied existence remains in the shadows virtually invisible to the larger world" (http://www.ala.org/awardsgrants/awards/339/select, para. 4).

Long before the #BlackLivesMatter movement began in the summer of 2013, Myers understood the importance of black lives being represented in the literature that young people read. He knew it mattered for black youth to see themselves reflected in the literature and for other readers to see them in the literature as well. As a proponent of the "We Need Diverse Books" (WNDB) campaign, Myers challenged diversity in the world of children's book publishing.

Just months before his death, Myers (2014 March 15) wrote an opinion piece for the *New York Times* exploring the question, "Where are the people of color in children's books?" This age-old question has been asked for decades as black images in children's books have historically been non-existent or fraught with stereotypes and negative portrayals (Martin, 2004; Sims, 1982). In his *NYT* article, Myers reprimands the publishing industry not only for a history of not representing people of color but also for not representing children from lower economic classes (para. 12). Myers addressed race *and* class in his work.

Likewise, Myers's son, Christopher Myers, wrote a parallel opinion piece for that same issue of the *New York Times* titled "The Apartheid of Children's Literature" (2014 March 15), in which he examined the exclusivity of characters of color and the impact this has on young people who struggle to dream beyond what they see as representations of themselves in books and media. He cited data on publishing trends in children's books from the Cooperative Children's Book Center (CCBC, 2018 February 28) and likened the lack of representation to relegating young people of color outside of the boundaries of imagination.

An example of this phenomena is when I have observed children role-playing around characters from the *Harry Potter* series and other books or movies from children's popular culture as they debate reasons the black playmates cannot "be" Harry, a particular Disney princess, or some superhero. Even in the wider sphere, some adults have expressed vitriol at the casting of black characters in roles they imagine as solely white such as *Little Orphan Annie* (Siddiquee, 2014 December 19) and Hermione in the Broadway production of "Harry Potter and the Cursed Child" (2017).

Yet, Hollywood has been blatant in its history of casting white actors in roles as Native American and continues to whitewash Asian stories in the film industry (Morgan, 2018 August 20). As Chimanada Ngozi Adichie (2009) eloquently points out, the danger of a single story is that it sends the message that some people have stories and others do not; some have stories worth telling and others do not.

Toni Morrison also addressed this concern by condemning master narratives as "whatever ideological script that is being imposed by the people in authority on everybody else." The mainstream narrative drowns out other narratives. Authors like Myers have worked to broaden choices in literature for children as a means of countering the damaging effects of master narratives (Moyers & Company, 1990 March 23).

Many of Myers's novels feature perspectives and problems that inner-city kids face (Johnson, 2012). The author's own struggles with figuring out race and navigating the blatant lack of book choices that related to his life experiences in high school are revealed in this quote from Myers's memoir, *Bad Boy* (2001): "Most of what I read and heard was negative. Blacks had always been slaves. Blacks had been lynched. Blacks could not eat at this place or that. There was little positive published about blacks except in the black press" (p. 138–139).

James Baldwin's story "Sonny Blues" (Baldwin, 1965) impressed Myers by portraying a black urban experience, giving him permission to write about his own experiences growing up in Harlem (p. 202). In "Where Are the People of Color in Children's Books?" article, Myers (2014, March 15) shared how reading was an integral part of most of his life. He recalled the search for his identity as a teenager, and while Myers enjoyed the stories he read in his youth, he was also keenly aware that something was missing. He needed more characters with whom he could identify, and lack of identifiable characters caused him to stop reading (para. 6).

Educator and critic Nancy Larrick explored the lack of diversity in children's literature in 1965 and wrote about it in her article titled "The All-White World of Children's Books." Importantly, she addressed the impact that the scarcity of diverse literature had on white children as well as children of color, touting that the disparity in representation can lead to white children believing they are "kingfish" while subtly being raised on small doses of racism dispensed in the books they read throughout their lives.

Myers's works of contemporary realism focused on making the lives of black children visible to young black readers; yet, his books also have appeal to a wide audience as evidenced by his numerous accolades. His efforts to promote diverse literature and be a voice for further inclusivity in the publishing world of children's books are valiant and essential. Fittingly, on March 18, 2016, We Need Diverse Books presented the first Walter Dean Myers Award, called "The Walter" Award, to honor "a diverse author whose work features a diverse main character or addresses diversity in a meaningful way" (We Need Diverse Books, 2015 September 29).

Librarian of Congress James S. Billington named Myers the National Ambassador for Young People's Literature for a two-year term in 2012 and 2013 with "Reading is not Optional" as his platform (Lamolinara, 2012, para. 1). The Ambassador promotes literacy and literature for young people on a national level. Knowing the benefits that reading can have on one's life and the far-reaching effects that can result from not reading, it is easy to understand why Myers would promote a stance that reading is not optional.

In the ever-growing landscape of YA literature, there is an even greater imperative to continue moving toward more inclusivity in children's and YA book publishing that offers diverse readers mirrors in which to see oneself accurately and fully represented; windows in which to view, appreciate, and respect the experiences of others; and doors through which to open and take action for social justice (Botelho & Rudman, 2009). Many thanks to Mr. Myers for his dedication to writing a lifetime of diverse stories for young people to enjoy.

CRITICAL DISCUSSION OF ONE MAJOR WORK AND PEDAGOGICAL FOCUS IN THE CLASSROOM

The *Autobiography of My Dead Brother* (2005) is a former National Book Award Finalist and is listed as one of ALA's Best Fiction for Young Adults. The book is geared for readers in grades 9–12 and contains instances of violence and characters engaged in gang/drug culture. Themes and concepts prevalent in the story center around family, friendship, loyalty, intrapersonal and interpersonal conflict, decision making, loss, hope, change, identity, and more. The protagonist and narrator of the story is fifteen-year-old Jesse, a black teen learning to navigate his life and the changes taking place around him in his Harlem neighborhood.

Jesse and Rise are two friends who grew up together in Harlem. They are such close friends that as small children they decide to become blood brothers like they saw two men do on an old television show. The two boys share similar interests and views on the world, until Jesse slowly realizes that Rise is changing. As a gifted artist, Jesse uses his drawing skills to document the way he views Rise's negative behavior as a metamorphosis into a person Jesse no longer recognizes.

Rise admires Jesse's artistic talent and asks him to write/draw his autobiography. As Rise sinks deeper into gang life and the drug culture that plague their Harlem neighborhood, Jesse has difficulty accurately depicting Rise in his artwork as the chasm in their relationship slowly grows larger and larger. After completing a picture that he thought made Rise look strange, Jesse thinks to himself:

> "You've become a different person," I imagined myself saying. "Somebody I almost don't know. That's why I drew you that way. You're not the same person I grew up with and who was my blood brother." (p. 135)

Jesse grows increasingly anxious about the constant drive-by shootings and funerals of young black men in his community. As a member of the Counts, a social group of the neighborhood teenage boys that operated as a nonviolent club, Jesse enjoyed hanging out with the other members, including Rise. When Mason, a renegade member of The Counts, gets into trouble and lands in jail, it leaves the group unsettled. A boy nicknamed Little Man tries to join the group, but the other members think he is too young and a bit of a wild card. Thus, they tell Little Man they will get back to him and subsequently dismiss him from the club location.

Meanwhile, Rise is demonstrating behavior and communicating a mindset that is not reminiscent of the person Jesse thought him to be. Formerly, Rise had been vocal about his disdain of drug dealers and the havoc they cause communities. To Jesse's bewilderment, Rise shifted his view to actively dealing drugs in the neighborhood. With Mason in jail, Rise wanted to take over as a rising star in one of the local gangs and own this new identity by behaving in ways that Jesse would have never conceived.

Jesse struggles to make sense of Rise's transformation, and he boggles things up when he tries to communicate with Rise about it. In addition to his drawings of Rise, Jesse creates a personal comic strip titled "Spodi Roti & Wise" in which the two characters have conversations reflective of the way he imagines his own discussions with Rise could be (p. 115). In the final comic strip segment that parallels the book's ending, only Spodi Roti is shown, alone, to ask rhetorical questions of Wise as he rests in peace (R.I.P.).

Ultimately, Rise's involvement in the gang escalates to a violent crescendo as police clamp down on anyone suspected of being connected with nefarious activities that have dogged the area. Several close calls for Jesse with drive-by shootings and a run-in with police leave him feeling scared, empty, and alone. On top of that, his father is going through his own personal crisis that results in a serious altercation between the two of them. A black cop who grew up in the neighborhood is working to steer Jesse and the other boys away from the dead-end life he knows is waiting for anyone lured by the fast money and façade of power in the gang world.

Rise is not listening, and Jesse is afraid for himself and his friend. As Jesse feels the loss of the childhood friend he used to know, real loss is realized when Little Man succumbs to the attraction of the gangs and shoots Rise before he has an opportunity to move with family to Miami as an attempt to temporarily escape the environment while things cool off in his neighborhood. Unfortunately, Rise's attempt is too little too late as his life is unexpectedly snuffed out. All of the childhood memories with Rise that Jesse held dear are infiltrated with the last moments of his friend dying in his arms.

Autobiography of My Dead Brother can be analyzed through several different lenses. Psychological literary criticism is one lens to use with this text to analyze a character's feelings, state of mind, personality traits, subconscious intentions, motivations, and unconscious fears or desires and how their behavior is dictated by these factors (Gillespie, 2010). The analysis could be approached using Freud's psychoanalytic theory in which the mind is a collective of id, ego, and superego battling each other in decision making based on desire or morality (Brief Books, 2016).

Moreover, Maslow's hierarchy of needs theory about human motivation is likely a relatable approach to psychological literary criticism for this text and its target audience. Adolescents can strongly relate to their own needs as well as the needs of others. Maslow's hierarchy of needs provides an organized framework from which readers can analyze Rise's behavior in *Autobiography of My Dead Brother*. As a humanist, Maslow's pyramid of needs relates to the whole person (Brief Books, 2016).

Teaching to the "whole child" is an approach in which educators not only address academic needs of students but move beyond the curriculum to a more holistic perspective that ensures children feel safe, secure, and valued within a school climate and culture that fosters the development of an effectively functioning and thriving democratic citizenry (Noddings, 2005). This concept relates to Maslow's hierarchy of needs and can be applied to an analysis of the needs Rise and other characters in *Autobiography of My Dead Brother* displayed.

The foundation of Maslow's hierarchy are physiological needs—the basic needs for survival such as clean air to breathe, water and nourishment, a roof over one's heads, and sleep. It is assumed that the main characters in the text had their physiological needs met, because Jesse and his friends hung out on front stoops of the homes they lived in, for example. The next level of the hierarchy of needs addresses safety, security, stability, and freedom from fear (Brief Books, 2016), among other needs. This is the main level of needs that posed a challenge for all of the characters.

For Rise, Jesse, and the other youth in their Harlem neighborhood, this level was grossly affected by the barrage of gun violence, gang activity, and drug abuse surrounding them. The ways in which the main characters internalized and responded to what was happening demonstrate attempts on their part to meet this level of needs—safety, security, and freedom from fear. Rise found security in the gang, but the amount of freedom he experienced is questionable because he had to always be watchful for retaliatory violence. To eliminate some of the fear of being a target, Rise felt he had to become the one doing the targeting.

Little Man had similar needs to Rise, but his motivation seemed to stem more from Maslow's level of "love and belonging." At this level, the hierarchy points to the need for friendship, affection, love, and intimacy (Brief Books, 2016). Little Man represents the longing for belonging, searching for any group to take him in and accept him regardless of the cost. Little Man's longing finally leads him to commit a crime that results in the loss of lives and futures.

On one hand, Rise was tired of waiting for his dreams to come true and weary of hoping for his situation to change only to continue to be disappointed when his train did not come in. This sentiment is illustrated in the "Spoti Roti & Rise" comic strip on page 76 of the novel. Rise (or Wise in the comic strip) is pontificating about the ethereal nature of dreams or of his hope to escape his reality. He so convinced himself that his dreams will never be realized that he does not notice when his train actually does come in, as seen in the last frame of the comic strip.

His choices—to see the train and get on board to a new and different destination—are right in his sight and depend on his decision to ride. Because it appears that Wise's eyes are closed throughout the comic strip, Spoti Roti cannot force him look at the train while it is approaching nor when it pulls into the station. On the other hand, Jesse has not given up hope that things can be better. He is challenged by all that is happening around him, but he is not hopeless and searches in anguish for relief from conflicting and confusing feelings related to the violence surrounding him.

Rise, Little Man, and Mason were all scrambling for ways to meet their needs for esteem. Esteem is the next tier of Maslow's hierarchy in which humans need independence, status, dominance, prestige, respect from others, and so forth (Brief Books, 2016). At one point, when Sidney takes Jesse and Rise to visit Mason in jail, there are unkind words and gestures exchanged between Rise and Mason. They get in each other's face as a standoff. Rise challenges Mason's authority and leadership on the streets, calling him out (pp. 59–60).

In this chest-to-chest confrontation, both young men were seeking respect from the neighborhood turf and from each other. They are both vying for dominance in the standoff, and this is clear to the reader and to Mason that Rise had plans to become the big man on the streets of their neighborhood. Mason ominously warns Rise:

> But the Counts are my peeps, and if you think you stepping into my shoes, you wrong. You just think about what you're hearing tonight. When you thinking of standing up against me, just remember that the only one of us that got something to lose is you because I don't care about a thing. Life don't mean nothing to me. (p. 62)

In Little Man's quest for status, he was willing to kill someone for acknowledgment, respect from the gang, and to feel dominance over a rival that was seemingly usurping power on the streets.

The final and utmost need according to Maslow's hierarchy is for self-actualization, or the ability to realize one's potential, to engage in personal growth, and to reach self-fulfillment (Brief Books, 2016). Sidney, the local cop on the beat, was the one character who was actively working to help Jesse and Rise sidestep some of the street drama in hopes that they would take a different path toward realizing their potential. Unfortunately, Rise was unwilling to listen to any of Sidney's logic.

Jesse was a talented artist. Jesse's fellow member of the Counts, Calvin, was a talented musician. There were likely countless other gifted young men and women in that neighborhood of which they were representative. Jesse and Calvin wanted to grow in their talents and even talked about it when it became clear that Rise was going to lead them both deeper into his entourage. Myers does not make known whether or not Rise had a particular skill or talent, but it is apparent that Rise had strong leadership skills that were wasted on criminal activity.

Autobiography of My Dead Brother (2005) is an effective text for applying principles of psychological literary criticism to study characters in depth (Gillespie, 2010). Moreover, the text offers many opportunities to delve into meaningful discussions and writing responses that can aid comprehension and enjoyment of the reading. The next section outlines ways in which teachers can use this text to meet the learning goals.

CLASSROOM ACTIVITIES OR INSTRUCTIONAL FOCUS

There are many opportunities for classroom use of the novel *Autobiography of My Dead Brother* (2005) that align with the Common Core State Standards for English Language Arts (CCSS-ELA). This text is leveled as 730L, or between 3rd- and 4th-grade reading level, according to the Lexile

Framework for Reading (MetaMetrics, Inc., 2018). Other sources list the text as 830L, which is 4th- to 6th-grade reading level (Scholastic, Inc., 2018). However, due to the content and mature themes in the text, Scholastic (2018) cites the text as geared for youth in grades 6–12.

The protagonist, Jesse, and his counterparts are mainly between the ages of fifteen and seventeen, or high school age. Thus, for purposes of the following pedagogical classroom focus, the activities discussed are aligned with the Reading Literature, Writing, and Speaking & Listening Standards for grades 9–10, which will focus on reading, discussion, and writing (http://www. corestandards.org/ELA-Literacy/RL/9-10/#CCSS.ELA-Literacy.RL.9-10.1).

The chapters of *Autobiography of My Dead Brother* are not numbered, but the reading can be divided into sections. For example, the book could be divided into five sections as follows: (a) p. 1–36, (b) p. 37–76, (c) p. 77–127, (d) p. 128–162, and (e) p. 163–213. As readers progress through the book, there are several approaches to the text that lend themselves to whole-class, small-group, and individual instruction. Some of the activities overlap. For instance, students may engage in individual writing in preparation for whole-class discussion.

Related standards for reading literature focus on determining theme(s) with the novel and how the theme(s) develop over the course of the story. Additionally, students can analyze how the main characters develop, interact with one another, and advance the plot or theme (RL.9–10.2; RL.9–10.3). Likewise, *Autobiography of My Dead Brother* is ripe with options for integrating writing, also. Students can complete a number of tasks that demonstrate their ability to "produce clear and coherent writing" (W.9–10.4) in which they are required to support with evidence from multiple credible sources (W.9–10.8).

In terms of speaking and listening, students can participate in a variety of discussions about the book's content to practice skills such as preparing for discussions, posing and responding to questions, building on others' ideas, and expressing one's own ideas clearly and persuasively (SL.9–10.1; SL.9–10.1A; SL.9–10.1C; SL.9–10.1D). Classroom connections for incorporating reading, writing, speaking, and listening are outlined for whole-class, small-group, and individual instruction.

WHOLE-CLASS INSTRUCTION

Prior to reading *Autobiography of My Dead Brother*, open with a warm-up or icebreaker survey of the class to find out how many students have biological or step-siblings. Have students share birth order and describe their relationship with their brothers and/or sisters as they feel comfortable. Jesse and Rise were not biological or step-brothers, but they were best friends growing up and felt like siblings until Rise began to change. Facilitate a discussion about friendships that may have been strong in elementary or junior high school that drifted apart by high school. Share reasons this may have occurred.

Also, before reading the book, ask students to pay attention to current events that relate to the story and bring in local or national articles to share with the class. Discuss the way in which the media portrays victims and perpetrators. Whose perspectives are represented in the articles? What questions does the article leave the reader asking? What background information might add understanding to the situations described in the articles? Are there certain trends in reporting style depending on which news outlet is reporting the incidents?

Set purpose for students as they read *Autobiography of My Dead Brother*. During reading, students create a character map to analyze the traits, thoughts, actions, feelings, and goals of either Rise or Jesse throughout the story using a graphic organizer. Their purpose for reading each section is to find clues to the nature of one of these two main characters. Students discuss whether or not they like the character and why or why not. Additionally, students reflect on what they would do or decisions they would make if they were in the character's situation.

After reading each section of the text, students complete the *Stop and Write* activity (McKnight, 2014, p. 67). This strategy helps students build writing skills while also aiding comprehension. Students use a two-column organizer to document their thinking (McKnight, 2014, p. 67). The first column is a summary of what the reader learned while reading. The reader records what they are thinking in the second column. In other words, the reader answers the question "What was this chapter or section about?" for the first column, and they write a personal reaction to what occurred in the second one.

During whole-class discussion, ask students what they are thinking about the section they just finished reading (Bomer, 2011). What connections did they make while reading (Bomer, 2011, p. 104)? Students might also engage in a debate or Socratic Seminar (Read-Write-Think, 2018, "Socratic Seminars"). Discussion questions might include: *Should you stand by your friends no matter what? Should Jesse have told his parents about the changes he noticed in Rise? What would you do if you noticed your close friend making poor decisions? What happens when people lose hope of a brighter future?*

SMALL-GROUP INSTRUCTION

Conflicts among the characters in *Autobiography of My Dead Brother* resulted in many challenges, difficult decision-making, and ultimately loss of innocence and life. The characters appeared to have no one with whom they could honestly confide. Though Sidney had grown up in their neighborhood and understood the pull of the streets on young black males, the boys did not consider him a trusted confidant because he was a police officer. Jesse had both parents in the household, but his relationship with his father was strained, and he did not want to add worry to his mother.

Use the classroom as a safe space in which to explore solutions to similar problems that Rise and Jesse faced. Ask students to work in small groups to identify some of the major conflicts of the characters in the story and discuss possible resolutions. Following the discussion, each small group should select different conflicts to act out. They should be tasked with providing a viable positive solution to the issue as part of the activity.

As another small-group activity, encourage students to research by exploring online resources from the Schomburg Center for Research in Black Culture and other pertinent websites and texts. Ask groups to focus on a particular era of the black experience in Harlem such as the Harlem Renaissance and the black experience in Harlem before World War I, blacks in Harlem before World War II, and blacks in Harlem from Civil Rights to present day. Student groups work together using Google Slides or other appropriate software such as iWork Suite or iMovie, Office Suite, Prezi, or other application to design a digital presentation to share their learning.

INDIVIDUAL INSTRUCTION

The "Stop and Write" writing activity, which was described in the Whole-Class Instruction section as preparation for the whole-class discussion, is one way to allow individuals to think about what they are reading on an individual level. According to McKnight (2014), this activity is a "Write to Learn" activity to help students develop their thinking and understanding of the text as well as provide a structure in which to examine and summarize the important aspects of a text (p. 68).

Another individual writing activity that also allows for creativity is RAFTS. RAFTS stands for *R*ole, *A*udience, *F*ormat, *T*opic, and *S*trong verbs. It is an adaptation of RAFT writing that highlights the use of descriptive action words. There are dozens of online templates and strategy use examples online. McKnight (2014) determined the RAFT strategy was effective in meeting several writing standards of the Common Core and in addressing the top four tiers of Bloom's Taxonomy: Application, Analysis, Synthesis, and Evaluation (p. 74). RAFT writing allows students to apply fundamental writing skills while merging creative and critical thinking.

For use with *Autobiography of My Dead Brother*, students take on the role of a character within the text and write to a particular audience (e.g., the police force, a trusted teacher or counselor, a parent, a best friend, a new boy moving into the neighborhood) using a format such as a poem, letter, diary entry, memo, news article, or script, to write about a particular topic related to the assigned reading. This type of writing requires students to understand the material they read at a deeper level and represent that deeper knowledge in a new and original way (McKnight, 2014).

INDIVIDUAL OR SMALL-GROUP OPTION

Finally, individual students create their own comic strip related to a theme from *Autobiography of My Dead Brother*. Artistically talented students may choose to create the comic free-hand. Others may want to use software such as Comic Life™ (https://plasq.com). Comic Life™ is comic-creation application available for the desktop, iPad, and iPhone that sets a comic overlay on photos. Students may also choose to work on their own, with a partner, or in a triad to create their comic strip.

This activity is fitting, because Jesse was a talented artist who not only drew pictures of Rise to document part of his life, but he also authored a comic strip titled "Spodi Roti & Wise" that occurred periodically throughout *Autobiography of My Dead Brother* as though it was part of Jesse's subconscious mind working out the personal conflicts with which he was challenged regarding his relationship with Rise and the ever-volatile and dangerous situation of living as a black male youth in his Harlem neighborhood.

In preparation for the comic strip activity, discuss the many themes in the story and ways that students might illustrate and represent a particular theme in their comic strip. To differentiate, students may choose an important scene from the book in which to create a comic strip. Share comic strips in class and have students determine the scene or the theme of each.

CONCLUSION

Walter Dean Myers was a giant in the world of YA literature. His passing on July 1, 2014, marked the end of decades of prolific writing for children and adolescents; yet, his legacy will be felt for many decades to come. Myers grew up in Harlem, and many of his stories are set in this locale, but he created relatable and memorable characters who grapple with authentic dilemmas and situations that many young people from many walks of life still confront today.

Autobiography of My Dead Brother represents one of those stories and is a milestone in YA literature. Explore Walter Dean Myers's work and delve into at least one of his many recognized selections to gain a greater understanding of who he was and what he cared about: telling a lifetime of stories for young people.

Bibliography of Works by Walter Dean Myers

Myers, W. D. (1969). *Where does the day go?* New York, NY: Bobbs-Merrill.
Myers, W. D. (1975). *Fast Sam, cool Clyde, and Stuff.* New York, NY: Viking.
Myers, W. D. (1977a). *Brainstorm.* New York, NY: Franklin Watts.
Myers, W. D. (1977b). *Mojo and the Russians.* New York, NY: Viking.
Myers, W. D. (1977c). *Victory for Jamie.* New York, NY: Scholastic.
Myers, W. D. (1978). *It ain't all for nothin'.* New York, NY: Viking.
Myers, W. D. (1979). *The young landlords.* New York, NY: Puffin Books.
Myers, W. D. (1981). *Hoops.* New York, NY: Delacorte.
Myers, W. D. (1982). *Won't know till I get there.* New York, NY: Viking.
Myers, W. D. (1984a). *Motown and Didi.* New York, NY: Viking.
Myers, W. D. (1984b). *The outside shot.* New York, NY: Delacorte.
Myers, W. D. (1987). *Crystal.* New York, NY: Viking.
Myers, W. D. (1988a). *Fallen angels.* New York, NY: Scholastic.
Myers, W. D. (1988b). *Scorpions.* New York, NY: Harper and Row.
Myers, W. D. (1990). *The mouse rap.* New York, NY: Harper and Row.
Myers, W. D. (1992). *Somewhere in the darkness.* New York, NY: Scholastic.
Myers, W. D. (1994). *The glory field.* New York, NY: Scholastic.
Myers, W. D. (1996). *Slam!* New York, NY: Scholastic.
Myers, W. D. (1999). *Monster.* New York, NY: Harper Collins.
Myers, W. D. (2000). *The greatest: The life of Muhammed Ali.* New York, NY: Scholastic.
Myers, W. D. (2001). *Bad boy.* New York, NY: Harper Collins.
Myers, W. D. (2003). *The beast.* New York, NY: Scholastic.
Myers, W. D. (2004). *Shooter.* New York, NY: Harper Collins.
Myers, W. D. (2005). *Autobiography of my dead brother.* New York, NY: Harper Collins Publishers.
Myers, W. D. (2006). *Street love.* New York, NY: Harper Collins.
Myers, W. D. (2008). *Game.* New York, NY: Harper Collins.
Myers, W. D. (2009). *Dope sick.* New York, NY: Harper Collins.
Myers, W. D. (2010). *Lockdown.* New York, NY: Amistad.
Myers, W. D. (2013). *Darius & Twig.* New York, NY: Harper Collins
Myers, W. D. (2015). *Juba! A novel.* New York, NY: Harper Collins.

REFERENCES

Adichie, C. N. (2009). Ted Global 2009: *The danger of a single story.* Retrieved from https://www.ted.com/talks/chimamanda_adichie_the_danger_of_a_single_story/transcript?language=en. May 6, 2018.

American Library Association (1996–2019). *Coretta Scott King—Virginia Hamilton Award for Lifetime Achievement.* Retrieved from http://www.ala.org/awardsgrants/awards/339/select.

Association of Illinois Middle Grade Schools (AIMS), (n.d.) About AIMS. Retrieved from http://aimsnetwork.org/about-aims/. April 26, 2018.

Baldwin, J. (1965). *Going to meet the man: Stories.* New York, NY: Vintage International.

Bishop, R. S. (2007). *Free within ourselves: The development of African American children's literature.* Portsmouth, NH: Heinemann.

Bomer, R. (2011). *Building adolescent literacy in today's English classrooms.* Portsmouth, NH: Heinemann.

Botelho, M. J. & Rudman, M. K. (2009). *Critical multicultural analysis of children's literature: Mirrors, windows, and doors.* New York, NY: Routledge.

Brooks, W. (2009). An author as a counter-storyteller: Applying critical race theory to a Coretta Scott King Award book. *Children's Literature in Education, 40*(1), 33–45.

The Brown Bookshelf (n.d.). Walter Dean Myers. Retrieved from https://thebrownbookshelf.com/?s=Walter+dean+myers

Cooperative Children's Book Center (CCBC). February 28, 2018 (last update). Publishing statistics on Children's/YA Books about people of color and first/native nations and by people of color and first/native nations authors and illustrators. Retrieved from https://ccbc.education.wisc.edu/books/pcstats.asp

Gay, G. (2000). *Culturally responsive teaching: Theory, research, & practice.* New York, NY: Teachers College Press.

Gillespie, T. (2010). *Doing literary criticism: Helping students engage with challenging texts.* Portland, ME: Stenhouse Publishers.

Harris, V. J. (1990). African American children's literature: The first one hundred years. *Journal of Negro Education, 59*(4), 540–555.

Johnson, V. (2012). *LibraryPoint Central Rappahannock Regional Library—Walter Dean Myers.* Retrieved from http://www.librarypoint.org/walter_dean_myers. April 26, 2018.

Lamolinara, G. (2012, January 2). *Walter Dean Myers named new national ambassador for young people's literature: Prolific author chooses "Reading Is Not Optional" as banner for platform.* Retrieved from https://www.loc.gov/item/prn-12-001/. April 18, 2018.

Larrick, N. (1965, September 11). The all-white world of children's books. *Saturday Review, 48,* 63–65. Retrieved from http://www.unz.com/print/SaturdayRev-1965sep11-00063/. April 26, 2018.

Library of Congress (n.d.). *National ambassador for young people's literature.* Retrieved from http://www.read.gov/cfb/ambassador/emeritus.html#a3. April 26, 2018.

Martin, M. H. (2004). *Brown gold: Milestones of African American children's picture books, 1845–2002.* New York, NY: Routledge.

McNair, J. C. (2010). Classic African American children's literature. *The Reading Teacher, 64*(2), 96–105.

MetaMetrics, Inc. (2018). Matching Lexile measures to grade ranges. Retrieved from https://lexile.com/educators/measuring-growth-with-lexile/lexile-measures-grade-equivalents/. May 2, 2018.

Morales, M. & Petersen, J. (2010 January 18). Walter Dean Myers inaugural recipient of the Coretta Scott King-Virginia Hamilton Award for Lifetime Achievement. Retrieved from http://www.ala.org/news/news/pressreleases2010/january2010/2010cskvirginiahamilton_pio. May 1, 2018.

Morgan, T. (2018 August 20). The history channel: Casting white people in Asian roles goes back centuries. Retrieved from https://www.history.com/news/yellowface-whitewashing-in-film-america.

Moyers & Company (1990 March 23). [Video interview and transcript]. Toni Morrison—part 2: Dealing with race in literature. Retrieved from https://billmoyers.com/content/toni-morrison-part-2/. May 2, 2018.

Myers, C. (2014, March 15). The apartheid of children's literature. *New York Times*. Retrieved, from https://www.nytimes.com/2014/03/16/opinion/sunday/the-apartheid-of-childrens-literature.html. May 1, 2018.

Myers, W. D. (2014, March 15). Where are the people of color in children's books? *New York Times*. Retrieved from https://www.nytimes.com/2014/03/16/opinion/sunday/where-are-the-people-of-color-in-childrens-books.html?_r=0. May 1, 2018.

Parker, K. N. (2008). My boys and my books: Engaging African American young men in emancipatory reading. In Brooks, W.M. & McNair, J.C. (Eds.), *Embracing, evaluating, and examining African American children's and young adult literature* (pp. 111–126). Lanham, MD: Scarecrow Press, Inc.

Noddings, N. (2005). What does it mean to educate the whole child? *Educational Leadership, 63*(1), 8–13.

Reading Rockets (n.d.). A video interview with Walter Dean Myers. Retrieved from http://www.readingrockets.org/books/interviews/myers

Read-Write-Think. (2018). *Strategy guide: Socratic seminars*. Retrieved from http://www.readwritethink.org/professional-development/strategy-guides/socratic-seminars-30600.html#research-basis

Rosman, K. (2017, October 10). In love with romance novels, but not their lack of diversity. *The New York Times*, Style section. Retrieved from https://www.nytimes.com/2017/10/10/style/romance-novels-diversity.html

Rowling, J. K. (2017). *Harry Potter and the cursed child*. New York, NY: Scholastic.

Scholastic, Inc. (2018). Scholastic book wizard: Autobiography of my dead brother. Retrieved from https://www.scholastic.com/teachers/books/autobiography-of-my-dead-brother-by-walter-dean-myers/. May 2, 2018.

Siddiquee, I. (2014, December 19). Why a black *Annie* is so significant. *The Atlantic*. Retrieved from https://www.theatlantic.com/entertainment/archive/2014/12/why-a-black-annie-is-so-significant/383894/. May 1, 2018.

Sims, R. (1982). *Shadow and substance: Afro-American experience in contemporary children's fiction*. Urbana, IL: National Council of Teachers of English.

Tatum, A. (2005). *Teaching reading to Black adolescent males: Closing the achievement gap*. Portland, ME: Stenhouse Publishers.

Walter Dean Myers. (2009). *Walter Dean Myers—reviews and awards*. Retrieved from http://www.walterdeanmyers.net/review.html

We Need Diverse Books. (2015, September 29). We need diverse books (WNDB) will present the first Walter Dean Myers award on March 16, 2018. Retrieved from https://diversebooks.org/we-need-diverse-books-wndb-will-present-the-first-walter-dean-myers-award-on-march-18–2016/. May 1, 2018.

Chapter 4

Virginia Hamilton, Liberation, and *Bluish*

Generating Acceptance and Empathy

Shanetia P. Clark and Steven T. Bickmore

Virginia Hamilton is an international treasure whose stories, as she stated, "come from my imagination, my memories, and all of the things that I know" (Open Road Media, 2011). Her work helped to shape children's and YA literature for multiple generations. Her catalog ranges from short story anthologies to picture books to novels. She wrote biographies, historical fiction, fantasy, folklore, science fiction, and contemporary realistic fiction. She is truly not only a trailblazer, but an author who acknowledges and honored the past. Her work is studied in classrooms, both K–12 and at the university level, around the world.

In 1975, Virginia Hamilton's novel *M.C. Higgins the Great* (1974) won the Newbery Medal, making her the first African American author to receive this honor. This book won "the grand slam of the Newbery Medal, National Book Award for Children's Books and *Boston Globe-Horn Book* Award. This feat has rarely been repeated" (Scholastic, 2019). Hamilton continued to garner awards and honors for her subsequent works.

Virginia Hamilton's work has been celebrated and garnered much critical praise. She earned honors such as the Hans Christian Andersen Medal, the Jane Addams Children's Book Award, the NAACP Image Award for Outstanding Literary Work for Children, and numerous honorary doctorate degrees. Her work has been named to be selected for state-level awards (Hamilton Arts, Inc., 2019). All of these awards give a glimpse into the esteemed impact of Hamilton's work and her place in the literary canon.

All of her works were anchored in aspects of familial connections and the larger questions of the time period. Virginia Hamilton's stories were influenced by her parents' storytelling. She reminisced about its influence. "My parents' accounts taught me a sense of community as well as the idea that there was more than one place to be in life. . . . I see a direct correlation between one's childhood days and nights and how these seemingly ordinary times, spaces, and places flourish in one's imagination" (Hamilton, 1999, p. 30).

Her imagination was sparked by her parents' stories and that imagination translated into her books. She viewed literature for young people much larger than words on the page; she insisted that "is important that the new millennium's children know how to think about the world they see. And we [as authors, illustrators, and publishers] can help them better understand the world by sharing our knowledge of children's literature" (Hamilton, 1999, p. 30). Continuing to keep Hamilton's work in the hands of today's students is one of the ways to help them remember the past and for them to find ways to meld it into their hopes and dreams of the future.

Virginia Hamilton anchored her stories in "the deep concern with memory, tradition and generational legacy, especially as they helped define the lives of American blacks from the days of slavery onward. Ms. Hamilton described her work as 'liberation literature'" (Fox, 2002). This literary stance must be invited into the classroom. Hamilton's quest, shared by the other three authors in this collection, has still gone largely unrealized when one considers the scarcity of books that represent people of color (Huyck & Dahlen, 2019) and other marginalized populations.

Liberation literature is important because it exposes children and adolescents "narratives that counter common negative stereotypes or omissions about people based on some identity characteristic (e.g. race, disability, gender, sexual orientation, economic status). Liberation literature *consciously* and *consistently* reinforces these counter-narratives" (Southern Poverty Law Center, 2019, emphasis added). Hamilton's work enables readers to confront negative stereotypes and characteristics. With this view of liberation literation, Hamilton strove to disrupt stereotypes of people who have been marginalized.

Inviting Hamilton's various works into the classroom and curricula, teachers and their students are exposed to robust characters. No longer are, for example, African Americans limited to be viewed as "the problem"; instead, they are seeing as the heroes and heroines who have escaped slavery or overcame other (horrific) events. Young readers are able to engage in "imaginative rehearsal" (Gallagher, 2009) by imagining themselves as the characters or going through similar situations in the text. They are able to move beyond the text and consider how these narratives could affect their lives.

The use of liberation literature ensures that texts used in the classroom are "windows, mirrors, and sliding glass doors" (Bishop, 1990) for all children. Liberation literature and counter-narratives are especially important tools to help young children develop understanding about different social identities and groups of people. Bishop said that liberation literature "allows the reader to be a witness to the protagonist's suffering and also triumph. Both the protagonist in the story and the reader are, therefore, liberated" (Open Road Media, 2014).

Hamilton's liberation literature emphasizes survival for the "whole soul" (Open Road Media, 2011). Her work tackles the injustices levied upon African Americans from slavery to the present. It also spoke to the realities of those discriminated based on gender, race, and ability. Hamilton's concept of liberation is demonstrated through the various vehicles through which she invites readers to experience empathy, curiosity, and freedom through her literature. This chapter will discuss Hamilton's last novel, *Bluish* (1999), and provide activities that may be used with individual students, small groups, or an entire class.

SUMMARY OF *BLUISH* AND ITS THEMES

This story is of a girl named Dreenie and her burgeoning friendship with a new classmate known as "Bluish." Her 5th-grade classmates call her Bluish—even though her real name is Natalie—due to the coloring of her skin. Bluish's skin appears "bluish" due to her leukemia and the resulting chemotherapy treatments. Her condition is an unknown as the novel begins and most students just see her as different. Dreenie and Tuli move past their fear and get to know the real Natalie. *Bluish* is an example of liberation literature for it tells the story of unpacking and disrupting stereotypes of race, gender, and ability.

Virginia Hamilton "focuses quite often on 'outsider' children—children who are different in some way from other children. They might be different in terms of color, or color differences might be blended with gender, class, or cultural conflicts that children are experiencing. . . . Or they might be wrestling with an interest, talent, preoccupation, or disability that sets them apart from other children or other family members" (Mikkelsen, 1999). *Bluish* is a perfect example of novel that explores this issue that runs through all of Hamilton's work.

Hamilton brings readers into the world of this 5th-grade class through two distinct narrative formats. The first is Dreenie's private journal, which is in first person, and the second is through a third-person point of view. The deliberate choice to go back and forth between first-person and third-person narrative enables readers to experience Dreenie's curiosity and navigation through her relationships with Tuli, Bluish (Natalie), and her life at school and with her family.

Readers are able to get a peek into Dreenie's mind as she attempts to bring outsiders into the fold. The first-person perspective provides readers with a unique glimpse into how an individual tries to puzzle out the right thing to do. Dreenie's journal serves as space for her to ask questions, to wonder, and to make sense of her world. The third-person technique gives readers the chance to step back and gain a larger understanding of the dynamics of this 5th-grade class and Dreenie's family.

Virginia Hamilton shared the following during an interview: "I would like to have teachers read and students read the book and talk about it," says Hamilton. "I know it's very difficult to know what writers mean, but I think the bottom line is what kids get out of it and how they relate to it, and I don't think that needs to be taught. To read books is to learn the process of storytelling, or what stories are and that stories make life logical" (Mikkelson, 1999).

Ideas for books are not only created in the mind of the writer. They pull ideas from their experiences and they explore situations and environments that help them create robust settings and character. Hamilton's creative process while writing *Bluish* can be instructive for students.

Hamilton spent time at the Manhattan New School (PS 290) in New York City to research *Bluish*. She visited with the classroom teacher and the 5th-grade students. She listened to the joys, fears, delights, and questions of 5th graders, their teacher, and the principal. Hamilton used her journalistic background to gather the authentic voices of these children and used them to anchor the story of Dreenie and her classmates.

In addition, she, as with all of her works, utilizes the tools of an anthropologist—primary sources, observations, interviews, and other narratives. She contextualized her stories within historical, social, and economic lenses. Hamilton embraced the way the oral tradition (storytelling) and intersectionality of class, race, gender, and socioeconomic status impacted on one another. *Bluish* works through storytelling and the intricate intersectionalities.

These practices that Hamilton employed can serve as a model for instructions that we can be used with students to develop individual, small-group, and whole-class activities. Using these activities, students will embark on amplifying the contextual grounding, narrative frame, and larger questions that are generated when students read and consider the themes presented in *Bluish*.

INSTRUCTIONAL ACTIVITIES

Instructional activities that are inspired by Virginia Hamilton and *Bluish* are detailed in the following sections. These lessons are aligned with the NCTE/ILA Standards. The astute teacher can modify these activities to match the specific needs and concerns of the students. In this case, *Bluish* is a novel more closely related to middle-grade issues and concerns and the activities here align most directly with their level of development.

INDIVIDUAL ACTIVITIES

Following Hamilton's model of observing in a classroom, teachers will guide students to be mini ethnographers. First, teachers will need to have students define and research key terms such as *anthropologist, primary sources, observations, interviews,* and *ethnographer.* After they gain an understanding of these terms, the teacher will create groups so that each group focuses on one of the terms. These groups will create a working definition of each term in order to become an expert.

Next, the teacher will rearrange the students into groups so that there is an expert for each term in the group. In other words, the students will share their working definitions in a jigsaw collaborative group. The jigsaw method helps build comprehension, encourages cooperative learning among students, and helps improve listening, communication, and problem-solving skills (Reading Rockets, n.d.). A solid understanding of these key terms serves as prerequisite for the small-group activity.

It should be noted that this is an activity that can be framed as a before-reading activity that would help students look closely at the community about which they will be reading. Indeed, if they are middle-grade students, Dreenie's classroom environment might be similar to their own. If positioned as an activity at the end of reading the novel, then the activity can prepare them to analyze closely the setting, the characters, and the themes they have been considering as they were reading.

SMALL-GROUP ACTIVITY

A lesson for the small-group activity is the writing of a conversation among an imagined group of friends. First, the teacher will have students conduct "field research" by listening to a group of people while they are in a setting like a mall, a restaurant, a park, or on public transportation. The students write a conversation or scene based on the group of friends in a specific location. They may consider questions that they think that Virginia Hamilton asked the 5th-grade class that inspired *Bluish*. These questions may inspire their "field research."

Other options for the guiding questions and considerations are listed here:

1. Collect snippets of conversations. Determine if there are signature quotes that embody the personalities of each group member.
2. Imagine how these friends would interact away from the setting where first seen. What if they were at a party? A show? In the classroom?

3. Consider how the change of place (the location) affects the dynamics of the friends group.
4. Make sure the conversation has tellability.

What makes a story tellable? Beach and colleagues (2006, p. 128) posit that "a story's tellability—what makes it worth telling—is that its *point* is not *in* the story, but is socially constructed by the teller and the audience in the storytelling event." Moreover, they advance the position that effective narratives highlight "extraordinary events by emphasizing violations of the norm—the fact that the *event was out of the ordinary*" (Beach, et. al, 2006, p. 127; Clark, 2011, emphasis added). This lesson may eventually be the precursor to a drama activity wherein the conversation is written as a one-act play and eventually performed.

WHOLE-CLASS INSTRUCTION

For this whole-class activity, the teacher will have the students collect lines or quotes that stand out in *Bluish*. The teacher will post these quotes on the board, and the students will use these as discussion starters. Guiding questions for these discussion starters are as follows:

1. Why does this quote stand out to you?
2. How does it advance the story?
3. In what ways does this quote connect to your life?
4. How does this quote align with a theme of the book?

The students may also use the quotes to as the inspiration for visual representations. The student must include the quote or significant line from the story in the visual representation. Some ideas for the visual representations include a collage, a portrait, or a sculpture. The students may select the media supports their vision. The teacher will host a gallery walk of the students' artwork. Each work must also have a title, a list of the media used for the visual creation, and an "artist's statement" (Hotchkiss, n.d.).

Since one of the major themes of the *Bluish* is the acceptance of others. There is another activity that might be added. Adolescents can often be cruel to each other, but at the same time have an intense sense of right and wrong when it affects them or those about who they know or care deeply. In the opening pages of the book, Dreenie records in her journal finding Bluish (Natalie) parked in the middle of the hall as students flood around her. Dreenie offers to move her out of the way, but Bluish responds, "I'm sitting right her until they look at me!" (Hamilton, 1999, p. 9). Bluish pronounces the desire of so many adolescents to be seen and acknowledged as they are.

For this additional activity the teacher would collect a series of images that reflect differences that are visual. It is also important to note that this might be done as an introductory activity after reading the first few pages of the book together, but it might also be done as a concluding activity to help focus student of the importance of accepting others and to help them develop the skills to do so.

The first image might be of an adolescent in a wheelchair. The teacher might then ask students how they might begin a conversation with such a person, how they might include them in an activity. Students can record their responses silently so that all participate. Then the teacher might ask students to share their suggestions as they are recorded on the board. To further advance the activity, the teacher would then show other images of adolescents that are different. Images might include someone with a significant scar, someone with a missing limb, someone wearing a hijab, someone wearing a turban, or a variety of other signifiers.

The class can discuss how to have conversations and activities that include those who don't immediately appear to be like they are. Differences are a reality. Responses to these differences are often culturally imposed and manipulated by the context. Students are often quite astute at recognizing what should be happening as opposed to what is happening. Such an activity would help the class create a culture and climate that would help them embrace the differences they find among each other and in the world in which they live.

CONCLUSION

Virginia Hamilton's legacy will continue to impact children's and YA literature. Her work implored readers to look at their world in profound ways. She used literature as a vehicle through which young people could learn about, question, wonder about, and seek positive change in society. She told robust stories that pushed young readers to be agents of change and courage.

List of Virginia Hamilton's Works Classified as for Adolescents

Hamilton, V. (1974). *M.C. Higgins, the great.* New York: Macmillan.
Hamilton, V. (1978). *Justice and her brothers* (1st ed.). New York: Greenwillow Books.
Hamilton, V. (1980). *Dustland* (1st ed.). New York: Greenwillow Books.

Hamilton, V. (1981). *The gathering* (1st ed.). New York: Greenwillow Books.

Hamilton, V. (1982). *Sweet whispers, Brother Rush*. New York, N.Y.: Philomel Books.

Hamilton, V. (1983a). *The magical adventures of Pretty Pearl* (1st ed.). New York: Harper & Row.

Hamilton, V. (1983b). *Willie Bea and the time the Martians landed* (1st ed.). New York: Greenwillow Books.

Hamilton, V. (1984). *A little love*. New York: Philomel Books.

Hamilton, V. (1985). *Junius over far* (1st ed.). New York: Harper & Row.

Hamilton, V. (1987a). *A white romance*. New York: Philomel Books.

Hamilton, V. (1987b). *A white romance* (1st HBJ/Odyssey ed.). San Diego: Harcourt Brace Jovanovich.

Hamilton, V. (1988). *Anthony Burns: the defeat and triumph of a fugitive slave*. New York: A. A. Knopf.

Hamilton, V. (1989a). *The gathering* (1st HBJ/Odyssey ed.). San Diego: Harcourt Brace Jovanovich.

Hamilton, V. (1989b). *Justice and her brothers* (1st HBJ/Odyssey ed.). San Diego: Harcourt Brace Jovanovich.

Hamilton, V. (1989c). *Willie Bea and the time the Martians landed* (1st Aladdin Books ed.). New York: Aladdin Books.

Hamilton, V. (1990). *Cousins*. New York: Philomel Books.

Hamilton, V. (1993). *Plain City*. New York: Blue Sky Press.

Hamilton, V. (1998). *Second cousins*. New York: Blue Sky Press.

Hamilton, V. (2002). *Time piece: The book of times*. New York: Blue Sky Press.

Hamilton, V., & Davis, L. (1990). *The dark way: Stories from the spirit world* (1st ed.). San Diego: Harcourt Brace Jovanovich.

Hamilton, V., & Hogrogian, N. (1969). *The time-ago tales of Jahdu*. New York: Macmillan.

Hamilton, V., & Keith, E. (1968). *The house of Dies Drear*. New York: Macmillan.

Hamilton, V., & Moser, B. (1991). *The all Jahdu storybook* (1st ed.). San Diego: Harcourt Brace Jovanovich.

Hamilton, V., & Pinkney, J. (1980). *Jahdu* (1st ed.). New York: Greenwillow Books.

Hamilton, V., & Shimin, S. (1967). *Zeely*. New York: Macmillan.

REFERENCES

Beach, R., Appleman, D., Hynds, S., & Wilhelm, J. D. (2006). *Teaching literature to adolescents* (2nd ed.). New York: Routledge.

Bishop, R. S. (1990, Summer). Mirrors, windows, and sliding glass doors. *Perspectives: Choosing and Using Books for the Classroom*, 6(3).

Clark, S. P. (2011). Guiding the noticing: Using a dramatic performance experience to promote tellability in narrative writing. *The Clearing House: A Journal of Educational Strategies, Issues and Ideas*, 85(2), 65–69. https://doi.org/10.1080/00098 655.2011.616918

Fox, M. (2002). Virginia Hamilton, writer for children, is dead at 65. Retrieved from https://www.nytimes.com/2002/02/20/arts/virginia-hamilton-writer-for-children-is-dead-at-65.html

Gallagher, K. (2009). *Readicide: How schools are killing reading and what you can do about it*. Portsmouth, NH: Stenhouse Publishers.

Hamilton, V. (1974). *M.C. Higgins, the great*. New York: Macmillan.

Hamilton, V. (1999, May). "Looking for America." *School Library Journal, 45*(5), 28–31.

Hamilton, V. (1999). *Bluish: A novel*. New York: Blue Sky Press.

Hamilton Arts, Inc. (2019). Awards and honors. Retrieved from http://www.virginiaha milton.com/awards/

Hotchkiss, S. (n.d.). How to write an artist statement. Retrieved from https://the creativeindependent.com/guides/how-to-write-an-artist-statement/

Mikkelsen, N. (1999). Discussion guide to the novels of Virginia Hamilton. Retrieved from https://www.scholastic.com/teachers/lesson-plans/teaching-content/ discussion-guide-novels-virginia-hamilton/

Open Road Media. (2011). Meet Virginia Hamilton. Retrieved from https://www. youtube.com/watch?v=AyP5ZOMEn6c.

Open Road Media. (2014). Virginia Hamilton on liberation literature. Retrieved from https://www.youtube.com/watch?v=0XjAx-KqHFw.

Reading Rockets. (n.d.) Jigsaw. Retrieved from https://www.readingrockets.org/ strategies/jigsaw.

Scholastic, Inc. (2019). Virginia Hamilton. Retrieved from https://www.scholastic. com/teachers/authors/virginia-hamilton/

Southern Poverty Law Center. (2019). Liberation literature and counter-narratives. Retrieved from https://www.tolerance.org/classroom-resources/teaching-strategies/ exploring-texts-through-read-alouds/liberation-literature

Chapter 5

These Tears Are Real

Historical Representations in Julius Lester's Day of Tears

Ruth McKoy Lowery and Cheryl Logan

History is not only an accounting of what happened when and where. It includes also the emotional biographies of those on whom history imposed itself with a cruelty that we can only dimly imagine.

—Julius Lester, 2005, p. 176

CRITICAL RECEPTION

The iconic author and storyteller Julius Lester is well known for his descriptive retelling of the past, particularly representing stories of the experiences of African Americans. The epigraph cited in Lester's *Day of Tears*, the 2006 Coretta Scott King author award winner, illuminates the importance the author places on history and its role in the lives of African Americans.

Stories matter. They are meaningful for every reader, helping them to see a thought or idea transformed from an author's mind to the pages of a book. Young adults often do not get to share their opinion about a story they read. They are asked to look at the literary merits of a book, to analyze the author's stance, or to dissect some section of a story often for a book report or answering questions for an examination.

However, Lester (2005b) determines that he wants "readers to become so involved in a book that the story becomes their story, regardless of the gender or race or the story's characters" (p. 29). Lester argues further that he wants them to be "emotionally invested" when they read stories, just as much as an author is emotionally invested when writing the story (p. 29).

Day of Tears (2005) is one of Lester's stories, geared toward an adolescent audience. It is a poignant tale of the casualties of slavery in the United States. A story that pushes the reader to dig deeper, eliciting an aesthetic and efferent understanding of the story (Spiegel, 1998). In the remainder of this chapter, we examine *Day of Tears*, arguing for how this poignant story can be used with adolescent readers, to stimulate a deeper understanding history and the role played by African Americans. We begin with a brief introduction to the author and end with several activities that can be integrated into a literacy curriculum.

JULIUS LESTER: AUTHOR AND EDUCATOR

Lester, born Julius Bernard Lester (January 27, 1939–January 18, 2018), is no stranger to the literature world. He has garnered several awards for his writing, including the Newbery Medal, the Coretta Scott King Award for authors and the Boston Globe-Horn Book Award. For over thirty years, Lester was an educator of Afro-American and Judaic studies. He was a noted educator, historian, folklorist, writer, and professional musician and singer in his early years (Vang, 2005). He retired in 2003 from the University of Massachusetts at Amherst.

Lester, the award-winning author, published "nearly 50 books, including works of nonfiction, fiction, memoir, and folklore as well as literature for young readers" (Langer, 2018, n.p.). Langer applauds Lester as "an intellectual explorer who in volume after noted volume chronicled African American life" (n.p.). With his recent passing, Lester leaves behind a strong body of work that will continue to inspire the reading audience for years to come.

WHY HISTORICAL FICTION?

Historical fiction is still a popular category in the YA fiction classification. Young readers are able to see the past through a lens that makes the story relatable. McArdle (2015) determines that historical fiction "has the ability to transport readers to another time and place, giving them a window to the past and the ways in which people lived, worked, fought, and loved" (p. 81). Lester certainly does this and more. He helps readers to see the deep truths that are sometimes glossed over in books about the past, particularly books about slavery.

Lester (2002) sees his body of work as paying "homage to the dead" (p. 57). He writes for the silent voices, those voices that were not heard when they were alive. Helping readers to see life in the past, the unadulterated concept of slavery and its baggage is sometimes hard to share. Parents and other gatekeepers of children's reading often sanction what students read. Thus, materials presented to children may tell a sterilized version of slavery and other African American experiences. Lester (2008) argues that although these folks are no longer alive, their voices do not have to be silent.

According to Thomas, Reese and Horning (2016), "Throughout the entirety of the history of the United States, African Americans have been active agents fighting for their own physical, social, and economic liberation from stifling oppression" (p. 7). Likewise, Anderson (2007) posits, "the dead have their lessons to teach us, if only we'll listen" (p. 20). Historical fiction, then, presents a version of the story that helps readers visualize what could have been, how it could have happened, and how it did happen. Lester plays an important role as a visionary author who presents stories of the African American experience in the United States to his readers.

Day of Tears: A Novel in Dialogue

Julius Lester's *Day of Tears* is an historical account of the Weeping Time. In March 1859 in Savannah, Georgia, the largest slave auction in U.S. history took place in order for Pierce Mason Butler, a prominent slave owner, to auction off 423 of his 450 slaves in order to settle his gambling debts. Written in dialogic form, Julius Lester eloquently captures the anguish, hatred, and humiliation of the slaves as they are ripped from their families and sold as chattel on an auction block in order to save their white slave master from his unpaid gambling debts.

POWER OF STORIES

According to Bishop (1990), books are sometimes windows, sliding glass doors, or mirrors that help readers to see the world in different ways. Through literature, the reader's experiences can be transformed in the way they see themselves and others. This reading experience also "becomes a means of self-affirmation, and readers often seek their mirrors in books" (Harris, 2007, p. 153). In *Day of Tears*, Lester skillfully presents a dialogue where readers get to step into the story and experience the anguish as slaves are sold off, some never to see their family members again.

Readers can experience this heartrending tale by gleaning a bird's eye view through a window, stepping through the door to embody what this experience meant for so many who suffered through slavery, or by gazing as if at a mirror to see a reflection of what this experience could have been. Through each character's voice, readers experience the atrocities of slavery.

Short (2011) finds that students learn to have conviction and courage about their own views as they also keep in mind the views and needs of others. They learn to do this through dialogue (p. 55). As each character shares his or her inner feelings about the horrible slave auction, the descriptive thunderous weather that settled over the town during this time gives strength to their testimonies of their recollections. In the opening lines, Mattie, Emma's mother, notes:

It's been three days since we've seen the sun. Yesterday it started raining and it hasn't stopped since. The rain is coming down as hard as regrets. Will said the rain started up just when the selling began. I ain't never seen a rain like this. Will said, "This ain't rain. This is God's tears." (p. 3)

This opening clearly sets the tone for the story that unfolds in *Day of Tears*.

An event that is so gruesome, many are sold, and few are left behind. The rain continues in torrential downpour until the last of the slaves are sold. An event guaranteed never to be forgotten because of the despicable pain it uncovers. Emma, sold off as a young girl, also reflects on this event many years later:

"I remember that morning like it was yesterday. . . . I can still hear the rain. It was so loud we had to almost shout when we had something to say to each other. . . . The rain was so hard and so loud it was like it was doing the grieving for us. . . . I ain't never seen a rain like that in all the years since, and that's been a lot of years." (p. 15–16)

As the reader delves further into the horror this "Day of Tears" represents, there is no question of why this event remains so imprinted on the characters' minds.

BEING CRITICAL THROUGH MULTIPLE LENSES

Short (2011) points out, "Literature provides the opportunity to make an emotional connection to particular characters, bringing together the heart and mind to create a sense of connection and a desire for action" (53–54). Reading critically must occur beyond the basic reading and liking or not liking a text. It means reading deeper to determine what makes a text reach to our deepest instincts soliciting our greatest responses. Being critical also means helping readers to look beyond the text in front of them to understand first the personal and second the wider impact that may exist (Creighton, 1997).

Stories can entertain, arouse curiosity, stimulate imagination, develop intellect, clarify emotions, attune to anxieties and aspirations, help recognize difficulties, and offer solutions to problems (Bettelheim, 1975). Creighton (1997) also posits that stories play a crucial role in the psychological, social, and cognitive development of the reader.

WHITENESS AS PROPERTY

Harris (1993) argues that the emergence of "whiteness as property" dates back to the origins of property rights in the United States. Whiteness as property is both a form of racial identity and a form of property. Harris articulates that the concept of "property" most common among theorists before the twentieth century includes the "rights" to intangible things. Hence, property is "a right, not a thing, characterized as metaphysical, not physical" (p. 1725). Whiteness as property then refers to the very existence of those who were, and are, considered white. It gave authority to do and be anything the "owner" wanted to do and be.

Annamma (2015) posits, "Whiteness was legitimized as property when being white was equated with permission to pursue genocide over and violent conquest of indigenous peoples" (p. 297). Being white was the asset that gave them rights and privileges above all other ethnicities. Gutierrez (2014) elaborates that although the meaning of "property" has changed over the years,

> whiteness and property share the same function—that of excluding those who do not own the same phenotype of those who are white. . . . This comes attached to the concept of white privilege, where those who own this skin tone are more prone to be given certain rights that "others" in society cannot have. (n.p.)

The privilege and rights enjoyed by whites or those passing as white enabled them to own land and people they felt were subordinate. It ensured they were the only ones to participate as active citizens and decision makers, without fear of reprisals. In *Day of Tears*, slaves are treated as chattel by whites. White owners, like Mr. Butler, had the right to sell humans as property to increase their monetary standing. Slaves on the Butler plantation were regarded as the "envy of all the slaves" because Mr. Butler's father treated them "almost like they was family" (p. 4). This increased the value of these slaves to competitive plantation owners.

When the current Butler owner amasses major gambling debts, his "only" recourse is to sell the valuable commodity in order to pay off his debt. He claims he does not want to sell the slaves, but he has no other choice. Mr. Butler's whiteness gives him the right to dehumanize the slaves, thus he sells them. As he sits and awaits the final sales of his slaves, he rationalizes that they probably have no feelings about what is happening to them. He takes their submissiveness by not fighting back as not caring for their loved one.

He argues, "Their emotions are not as refined as ours. Things that would hurt a white man or woman don't affect them. If anybody tried to take my Sarah or Frances away from me, I think I would kill them" (p. 19).

Sarah is emotionally attached to Emma, especially since her mother has left the family because she does not agree with the practice of slavery. Sarah reasons, "She holds me tight like Mama used to. I hold on to her like there's nobody left in the world except us. No one else here knows what it's like to be me except Emma" (p. 36). She is unaware that her father resents the close bond she shares with Emma. When Mattie implores him to leave Sarah home with Emma, Mr. Butler refuses, secretly thinking, "Emma acts too much like she's the girls' mother. . . . I will not have my oldest daughter turn into a copy of her mother. I won't!" (p. 43).

Mr. Butler wants to guarantee that Sarah won't grow up to be sympathetic to the slaves like his estranged wife. Thus, although he says he is not interested in selling Emma, he does not stop the slave-seller from seeking out a fair price for her. He notes, "Coming back from the auction yesterday, Weems asked me if I'd be interested if he could get a good price for Emma. I told him no, but I said it in such a way that Weems knew I meant maybe" (p. 43). At the slave auction, Sarah is certain that Emma will return home with her. When she realizes that this may not be true, she posits, "Emma? Papa wouldn't sell you. I know he wouldn't do that" (p. 85).

Will, Emma's father, beseeches Mr. Butler not to sell Emma as he bargains with him, "No! No! Master, you promised! You promised! You promised! . . . How could you do this? We grew up together. We was like brothers! How could you do this?" (p. 87). Butler's callous reply solidifies the difference in their positions, "But we aren't brothers, Will!" (p. 87). Although the two men had played together as children and Will had even saved Butler from drowning, he is quickly reminded that they were not equal. Like Emma, Will could easily be sold to the highest bidder.

The slaves quickly learn that their master's words cannot be trusted. Will is disappointed to find that this is true for his family: "Master say he wasn't going to separate husbands from wives and parents from their children. He must've forgot, 'cause he sold my sister and her husband to a master from Tennessee, and their daughter was bought by a lady from Mississippi'" (p. 9). This disregard for humanity permeates all sales during this horrible slave auction.

Emma's sale creates a rift in the family and Sarah refuses to forgive her father. As she grew into a young woman, Sarah is happy when her father tells her that she was "Mama's child and not his" (p. 109). She affirms, "I wished Emma had been there to hear him say that about me." (p. 109). Like her mother, who leaves the plantation and by extension the family, Sarah loathes slavery and later refuses to associate with her father. After she has a daughter, Sarah names her after her "friend" Emma, whom she is unable to forget.

Sarah never accepts the practice of slavery and even as her father was dying many years later, she wrestles to forgive him for the despicable act of selling Emma. Mr. Butler seeks Sarah's forgiveness in his final hours:

"Do you love your papa, Sarah?" he asked, his voice so weak I could barely hear him. All I had to do was not my head. I didn't even have to say anything. Just a simple nod and he would've died happy. But I wanted him to feel what Mattie and Will felt when he sold Emma. He looked at me, his eyes pleading. I took his hand in mine and patted it lightly and then left the room.

Sarah never embodies the notion of whiteness as property; however, she realizes that she still had choices Emma and other slaves did not and that even as she mourned how they were treated, she still had a more privileged life simply because of her whiteness.

Like Sarah, Emma reminisces about this period of her life in her later years. She now lives in Nova Scotia and has children and grandchildren. She wishes her parents could see that she escaped slavery and has built a good life for her family. Emma admonishes her granddaughter who is writing a school report about her grandmother:

And you be sure to put in that report of yours that I named your mother Sarah for a little white girl who hated slavery, too. She hated wrong and that's because she had a good heart. And that's all that matters in this life. If your heart hurts when you see somebody suffering, you have a good heart. (p. 170)

Discussion and Response Activities in the Classroom

Lester (2005) suggests that authors are not the only authority of the meaning contained within their books. It is quite possible that there are hidden meanings that the author may not even be aware. Lester asserts that students' meanings are just as important as the author's meaning. Students brings to their reading their own subjectivity, which renders a different meaning for each of them. These activities have the potential to yield a deeper understanding of the wealth of knowledge, skills, and intellect of a people who have been labeled ignorant, and incapable of feeling and learning.

Providing students with a plethora of books on different topics and allowing them to read and reflect on said books can garner deeper understandings about their lived world. The following activities serve as opportunities for discussion, reflection, and response to thought-provoking discussions about *Day of Tears*.

LITERATURE CIRCLES

Literature circles provide students with a guide for engaging in meaningful discussions about texts (Daniels, 2002). Students are separated into groups of four or five. They select a role that they will assume as they read the text.

Sample roles include a discussion director who leads the group discussions, a connector who helps to find connections between the story and experiences around them, a vocabulary enricher/word wizard who notes unfamiliar words as they read and later brings up these words for discussion after finding the meaning(s) of the words.

To create meaningful discussions as they read, students should rotate through the various roles embracing the opportunity to engage with the texts for a variety of purposes. Students determine how much of the text will be read, and the role of each group member prior to discussion. Each student will prepare to discuss his or her role. Students repeat the process and select different roles until novel reading and discussion are completed.

Table 5.1   Sample Literature Circle Roles

Group Members	Roles	Tasks
1	Director/discussion leader	Your job is to keep the group on task during text discussion. Come with questions, points, or wonderings that can help you to do this.
2	Passage picker	Your job is to select portions of the text you found interesting that you can use to lead group discussions.
3	Artist/illustrator	Your job is to create mental pictures for the others in your group to imagine or draw a picture of something that stands out for you in the text.
4	Connector	Your job is to connect the text to your lives, other students' lives, others around you, and the greater world.
5	Critic/researcher	Your job is to look critically at the text. Look at the "so what?" "what ifs?" of the themes in the text.
6	Summarizer	Your job is to prepare a brief summary of the reading. Begin the discussion with a short one- to two-minute statement that covers the key points, main highlights, and general idea of the text.
7	Travel tracer	Your job is to carefully track where the action takes place during discussion of the text. Describe each setting in detail, either in words or with an action map or diagram.
8	Word Finder/ Vocabulary Wizard	Your job is to be on the lookout for words to enrich your discussions. This can include words that have special meaning, puzzling or unfamiliar words, or words used repeatedly in the text.

Source: Teachers and students can select the five roles they want to use for each literature circle, depending on the age group and books being read.
Adapted from: Daniels, H. (2002). *Literature circles: Voice and choice in book clubs and reading groups.* Portland, ME: Stenhouse.

HISTORICAL SCAVENGER HUNTERS

Working in pairs, students embark on an archival data hunt to see how history records events such as slave auctions, slave ownership, and even bills of sale that often record the price and value of a slave. Students can access information in their local or school library, or the Internet. What information is recorded? How is the information recorded? How are individuals described in the records? Are they recognized as individuals or as property? How do libraries archive these historical materials? How different is the retelling today? Who is doing the telling/retelling?

Students can then compare the materials they find to Lester's description of the slave auction. They organize their collected notes and share with their classmates in small-group or whole-class presentations.

COMMUNITY CULTURAL WEALTH REPORTERS

In this activity, each student selects a character from *Day of Tears*. Drawing on Yosso's (2005) six forms of capital cultural wealth that are prevalent among people of color, students prepare a character sketch of one of the marginalized characters to discuss with their peers. These six forms include aspirational wealth, social wealth, familial wealth, linguistic wealth, navigational wealth, and resistant wealth (box 5.1).

BOX 5.1   COMMUNITY CULTURAL CAPITAL WEALTH

- **Aspirational capital**—the ability to maintain hopes and dreams for the future, even in the face of real and perceived barriers.
- **Social capital**—networks of people and community resources. These peer and social contacts can provide both instrumental and emotional support to navigate through society's institutions.
- **Linguistic capital**—the intellectual and social skills attained through communication experiences in more than one language and/or style.
- **Familial capital**—cultural knowledge nurtured among familia (kin) that carry a sense of community history, memory and cultural intuition. This form of cultural wealth engages a commitment to community wellbeing and expands the concept of family to include a broader understanding of kinship.

- **Navigational capital**—skills of maneuvering through social institutions. The ability to maneuver through institutions not created with Communities of Color in mind.
- **Resistant capital**—knowledge and skills fostered through oppositional behavior that challenges inequality.

Source: Adapted from: Yosso, T. J. (2005). Whose culture has capital? A critical race theory discussion of community cultural wealth. *Race Ethnicity and Education, 8*(1), 69–91.

Each student selects a marginalized character in *Day of Tears* and creates a character sketch of that individual using Yosso's (2005) six forms of capital cultural wealth. Ensure each character is selected and no more than three students select the same character.

a. Same characters come together and share their findings. Compare how each student portrays the character. Students may add information to their character sketch as they glean various perspectives as their classmates share their work.
b. Groups with one of each character come together to share their findings. In these small groups (four or five members), each student will share their character and their capital wealth within the group.
c. Whole-class share. Students discuss how this research and multiple discussion sessions impact their understanding of the slaves in *Day of Tears.*
d. Students complete "I Am" poems after all the discussions—students use the information from the cultural capital wealth sketch to complete the "I Am" poem. Use one of many formats readily available by doing a Google search.

MOVIE TRAILER

After reading *Day of Tears* and participating in various extension activities, students create movie trailers of their best interpretation of the story. In pairs or small groups of three or four, students pretend they have been selected to produce and direct a major motion film about *Day of Tears.* They then create a short movie trailer about a major issue or theme in this novel.

Students select seven to nine images they would use to depict specific themes, events, settings, or characters in the story. They then select a soundtrack for each chosen image. Ensuring that the soundtrack compliments the image and supports the message they wish to convey, they then set each image to the selected soundtrack. At the end of the book trailer, each group provides a brief explanation of the images and music selected, and the messages they intended to convey. The trailers can be presented as a culminating activity shared by the entire class.

CONCLUSION

Encouraging students to adopt a critical understanding of the stories helps them to adopt a questioning stance as they work toward changing their view of themselves and the world (McDaniel, 2004). Through critical conversations, teachers help students navigate through discussions about power and social justice issues. They learn how systems of meaning in society position them and others. Such conversations engender awareness of the structure of cultural systems and positions of power around them. Further, they can develop an awareness of how these systems can positively or negatively affect groups or individuals (Leland et al, 1999).

Day of Tears is a pivotal text to help readers accomplish these feats. The conversations are sometimes difficult, yet necessary to deepen readers' understandings of what it means to delve deeply into a topic or an issue of importance. Open dialogue means leaving no "stones unturned" as students seek to gather new evidence, information they can share with their peers and others. This openness helps them to see that no topic is taboo, and they are free to ask questions and delve deeper to understand deeper truths.

Bishop (2012) argues that it is important that children who have historically been ignored or ridiculed in stories see themselves portrayed visually and textually as realistically human. It is important for readers to live vicariously through the stories they read. For many, slavery is not a present-day reality for most Americans, but it does exist in the world today. However, we can never forget that it is important to be humane. To think kindly of others. To share the space we live in with others. To treat others as they want to be treated. Yokota (2009) reminds readers that through books, they can begin to know the world around them. This can include action.

Historical fiction brings the past to life in the eyes of young readers. Helping them see how stories are told and retold through various lenses can help them to actualize their vision of what the world was, is, and could be. Lester (2005b) determines that it is not enough to read and critically analyze his texts. More importantly, he is interested in knowing, "What did the book mean to you? Did it touch your soul?" (p. 31). Reading *Day of Tears* with a critical reader's lens does just that. It touches the depth of the soul and brings its readers to tears.

REFERENCES

Anderson, M. T. (2007). Printz Award honor speech. *Young Adult Library Services, 6*(1), 20–21.

Annamma, S. A. (2015). Whiteness as property: Innocence and ability in teacher education. *Urban Review, 47*, 293–316. doi: 10.1007/s11256-014-0293-6

Bettelheim, B. (1975). *The uses of enchantment.* New York, NY: Alfred A. Knopf.

Bishop, R. S. (1990). Mirrors, windows, and sliding glass doors. *Perspectives, 1*(3), ix–xi.

Bishop, R. S. (2012). Reflections on the development of African American children's literature. *Journal of Children's Literature, 38*(2), 5–13.

Creighton, D. C. (1997). Critical literacy in the elementary classroom. *Language Arts, 74*(6) 19-26.

Daniels, H. (2002). *Literature circles: Voice and choice in book clubs and reading groups.* Portland, ME: Stenhouse.

Gutierrez, D. (2014, February 14). Analysis of *whiteness as property* by Cheryl I. Harris. Retrieved from https://gutier27.wordpress.com/2014/02/14/analysis-of-whiteness-as-property-by-cheryl-i-harris/

Harris, C. I. (1993). Whiteness as property. *Harvard Law Review, 106*(8), 1707–1791.

Harris, V. J. (2007). In praise of scholarly force: Rudine Sims Bishop. *Language Arts, 85*(2), 153–159.

Langer, E. (2018, January 23). Julius Lester, whose literature explored African American life, dies at 78. *The Washington Post.* Retrieved from http://wapo.st/2n4tjTC?tid=ss_mail&utm_term=.4f792ba984cf

Leland, C., Harste, J., Ociepka, A., Lewison, M., & Vasquez, V. (1999). Exploring critical literacy: You can hear a pin drop. *Language Arts, 77*(1), 70–77.

Lester, J. (2000). Re-imagining the possibilities. *Horn Book Magazine, 76*(3), 283–289.

Lester, J. (2002). The way we were. *School Library Journal, 48*(1), 54–57.

Lester, J. (2005). *Day of tears: A novel in dialogue.* New York, NY: Disney.

Lester, J. (2005b). On the teaching of literature. *English Journal, 94*(3), 29–31.

Lester, J. (2008). Silent voices. *Horn Book Magazine, 84*(5), 537.

McArdle, M. M. (2015). Historical Fiction. *Library Journal, 140*(20), 81.

McDaniel, C. (2004). Critical literacy: A questioning stance and the possibility for change. *The Reading Teacher, 57*(5), 472–481.

Short, K. G. (2011). Children taking action within global inquiries. *The Dragon Lode, 29*(2), 50–59.

Spiegel, D. L. (1998). Reader response approaches and the growth of readers. *Language Arts, 76*(1), 41–48.

Thomas, E. E., Reese, D., & Horning, K. T. (2016). Much ado about *a fine dessert*: The cultural politics of representing slavery in children's literature. *Journal of Children's Literature, 42*(2), 6–17.

Vang, M. (Ed.), (2005). *Something about the author. 157.* Detroit, MI: Gale.

Yokota, J. (2009). Asian Americans in literature for children and young adults. *Teacher Librarian, 36*(3), 15–19.

Yosso, T. J. (2005). Whose culture has capital? A critical race theory discussion of community cultural wealth. *Race Ethnicity and Education, 8*(1), 69–91.

Chapter 6

The Early Reception of Mildred D. Taylor's *Roll of Thunder, Hear My Cry*

Chris Crowe

CRITICAL RECEPTION

Winner of the 1977 Newbery Medal for *Roll of Thunder, Hear My Cry*, Mildred D. Taylor was a beneficiary of efforts to encourage diversity in books for young readers. Decades before the current #WeNeedDiverseBooks campaign, some in the children's book world, including the Council on Interracial Books for Children (CIBC), sounded the alarm about racial homogeneity and hegemony in children's literature. The push wasn't directly related to the 1960s Civil Rights Movement, but the increasing awareness of racial inequality surely prompted teachers, librarians, and publishers to consider books from a different, more balanced perspective.

In 1965, former International Reading Association president Nancy Larrick published what may have been the initial catalyst for greater inclusion in children's publishing. "The All-White World of Children's Books" appeared in the September 11 issue of the *Saturday Review*, and it turned a spotlight on the appalling lack of diversity in children's books and the potential negative impact such a lack might have on young African American readers. For her article, Larrick reviewed more than 5000 children's books published in 1962, 1963, and 1964.

Here's what she found:

Of the 5,206 children's trade books launched by the sixty-three publishers in the three-year period, only 349 included one or more Negroes—an average of 6.7 percent. Among the four publishers with the largest lists of children's books, the percentage of books with Negroes is one-third lower than this average. These four firms (Doubleday, Franklin Watts, Macmillan, and Harper & Row) published 866 books in the three-year period, and only 4.2 percent have a Negro in text or illustration. Eight publishers produced only all-white books. (Larrick, p. 64)

She went on to point out that the statistics were the barest of all measures of diversity. More careful review of the books showed that they perpetuated racial stereotypes or relegated black characters to minor or background roles or whitewashed the true reality of racism as experienced by African Americans at the time. Larrick ended her article with a simple, yet powerful, observation: "White supremacy in children's literature will be abolished when authors, editors, publishers, and booksellers decide that they do not need to submit to bigots" (p. 85).

Not coincidentally, in the same year, 1965, a progressive group of authors and illustrators, teachers, publishers, and parents established the CIBC, an organization dedicated to "promote a literature for children that better reflects the realities of a multicultural society." The Council, according to Larrick, hoped that "given encouragement, authors and artists will create good children's books that include nonwhites, and that given the manuscripts, publishers will produce and market them" (p 85).

Walter Dean Myers was one of the first African American authors to benefit from the CIBC's initiative, and in 1986 he wrote, "I felt proud to be part of this new beginning. . . . I understood, and I know the others did too, that it was not only for black children that we wrote. We were writing for the white child and the Asian child too."

In a 2014 *New York Times* article, Myers said that as a young man, he

> needed more than the characters in the Bible to identify with, or even the characters in Arthur Miller's plays or my beloved Balzac. As I discovered who I was, a black teenager in a white-dominated world, I saw that these characters, these lives, were not mine. I didn't want to become the 'black' representative, or some shining example of diversity. What I wanted, needed really, was to become an integral and valued part of the mosaic that I saw around me (Myers).

Myers's early success paved the way for others to follow, including Mildred D. Taylor.

Taylor's first book, *Song of the Trees*—a prequel to *Roll of Thunder, Hear My Cry*—won the CIBC Award in 1973 and launched her writing career. *Roll of Thunder* published in 1976, and although it would win the 1977 Newbery Medal, its initial, myopic reviews, like the one in *The Times Literary Supplement* that opined, "Technically, however, this book is disappointing" (Stones), failed to anticipate that the novel would go on to win several awards, be translated into dozens of languages, and be a best-seller for decades.

School Library Journal acknowledged the book's poignant and personal representation of racism but panned the story for its underdeveloped characters: "In fact, the indignities and injustices suffered by her people and focused upon at such length and with such intensity that readers never really discover who the Logans are or how they've changed by virtue of their struggles" (Stenson, p. 140).

Kirkus recognized the novel's most prominent and praised attributes, the presence of a unified, loving family: "though the strong, clear-headed Logan family is no doubt an idealization, their characters are drawn with a quiet affection and their actions tempered with a keen sense of human fallibility" (Kirkus Reviews). Fritz's review in *The New York Times* also noted the quality of the Logan family: "They do what they have to do—indirectly, if possible. Of course, this may not always be possible, but if anyone can overcome, the reader knows it will be the Logans" (Fritz).

The *Horn Book* praised Taylor's novel: "The book presents injustice and several ways of dealing with it. . . . The events and settings are presented with such verisimilitude and the characters are so carefully drawn that one might assume the book to be autobiographical, if the author were not so young" (Holtze, 1976, 627). Writing in *English Journal*, Alleen Pace Nilsen (1977) considered the novel a junior high book because of the age of the protagonist. "However," she said, "the book is so well written, and there is still such a shortage of good books which authentically document the Black experience in America, that some high school librarians might also wish to order it" (p. 87).

Perhaps the most negative review appeared in England's *The Times Literary Supplement*:

"Technically, however, this book is disappointing. The mechanics of the first-person narration are clumsily handled: new stereotypes are created in Cassie's overly noble black parents and the evocation of the 1930s has a distinctly 1970s flavour" (Stones, p. 1415). But the reviewer had to admit that the novel still had merit "for the perspective it affords on racial issues, this book deserves to be widely read" (p. 1415).

After winning the Newbery Medal, *Roll of Thunder* soon found its way into classrooms and libraries throughout the United States. As most book reviewers did, teachers and librarians in the late 1970s valued its authentic portrayal of racism, but as the novel reached an ever-growing audience, readers also appreciated Taylor's portrayal of an African American family. In her Newbery acceptance speech, Taylor expressed that one of her goals in writing the novel was to portray the effects of racism, but also to show how a unified family survived racism. She hoped that her books will one day be instrumental in teaching children of all colors the tremendous influence that Cassie's generation–my father's generation–had in bringing about the great Civil Rights movement of the fifties and sixties. Without understanding that generation and what it and the generations before it endured, children of today and of the future cannot understand or cherish the precious rights of equality which they now possess, both in the North and in the South. If they can identify with the Logans, who are representative not only of my family, but of the many Black families who faced adversity and survived, and understand the principles by which they lived, then perhaps they can better understand and respect themselves and others. (pp. 407–408)

Twenty years later, in her acceptance speech for the ALAN Award from the Assembly on Literature for Adolescents of the NCTE (ALAN), she reiterated that in her novels, she wanted to present "a family united in love and self-respect, and parents, strong and sensitive, attempting to guide their children successfully, without harming their spirits" (Taylor).

Throughout her career, critics, teachers, and award committees recognized Taylor's success in accomplishing her goals. In 2003, she won the inaugural NSK Neustadt Award for her body of work, and in a tribute essay shared at the awards ceremony, critic Robert Con Davis-Undiano wrote that

[Taylor] is a writer whose work has marked a huge cultural shift in the lives of many American families who have suffered the indignities of poverty and racial discrimination. Taylor has been the quintessential social critic—better yet, social-studies teacher—introducing morality and social awareness in American schools for almost three decades, thus helping to eradicate, in Nancy Larrick's words, "the all-white world of children's books." (p. 11)

It's clear that Taylor's novel has not only stood the test of time but thrived across the decades.

CRITICAL DISCUSSION OF THE WORK

Set in Mississippi in 1933 and narrated by nine-year-old Cassie Logan, *Roll of Thunder* tells the story of the Logan family and their small community of African American sharecroppers who endure dire poverty and relentless racism. The black school children walk miles to attend a dilapidated and neglected elementary school and most mornings, they have to dodge the school bus filled with white children that barrels down the road on its way to a far superior school. Fear permeates the African American community because white vigilantes, "night men," recently burned three African American men for allegedly looking at a white woman.

This assault is just one of many racial incidents in the book. For being outspoken and "uppity," Cassie's mother loses her teaching job and the lost income puts the Logan land at risk. Cassie has problems of her own, including Lillian Jean Simms, a racist white girl. A major plot element involves Cassie's brother's friend, T. J. Avery, a needy troublemaker who becomes tragically involved with two older, racist white boys. The personal and community trials the Logans face show them at their noble best: a family unified by love, courage, and faith.

Cassie's parents play major roles in the novel. The family relies on their father's strength, patience, and wisdom, and in crucial scenes, Cassie's mother lovingly dispenses advice and comfort. The story's various conflicts—primarily caused by racism and poverty—require the Logan children to learn important lessons about life and themselves.

Taylor excels at putting her characters in situations that represent what life was like for poor African Americans in Mississippi in the 1930s; scenes involving her villainous characters and their vile ways are some of the most memorable moments in the novel.

Taylor also shows the crushing, dispiriting weight of poverty people endured during the Depression. By the end of the book, readers have a clear, personal sense of how difficult life must have been for poor Mississippi farmers and sharecroppers. Taylor received consistent praise for her honest portrayal of the harsh realities of the time. The conflicts resulting from the combination of the hopeless economic situation with the toxic racist environment become essential threads throughout the plot of *Roll of Thunder*.

The many strengths of Taylor's novel, including the still-relevant connections to racism in America, have made it a true YA classic.

POTENTIAL PEDAGOGICAL FOCUS
IN THE CLASSROOM

There are many reasons *Roll of Thunder, Hear My Cry* has been a popular classroom text for more than forty years. First, just as Pam Muñoz Ryan's *Esperanza Rising* provides a Latino perspective to life in the Great Depression, Taylor's novel shows how African Americans in the South lived during the 1930s. The Logans' story reveals the economic hardships endured by blacks in the Deep South during the Depression and shows how Jim Crow racism compounded their suffering.

The novel also disrupts many African American stereotypes. In the introduction to the fortieth-anniversary edition, she wrote that Taylor had wanted to present "a family united in love and self-respect, and parents, strong and sensitive" (p. vi). Cassie's family is unified, educated, and hardworking, and they are led by a strong father figure. Because they live in a society dominated by Jim Crow politics, the Logans are victims of racism, but their courage and unity give readers optimism that this family will not be crushed under the burden of white supremacy.

Roll of Thunder is also an excellent example of historical fiction. Taylor weaves historical details from the 1930s with details from her own family history, and could serve as a model for students to write their own brand of historical fiction. These qualities provide a springboard to classroom discussions about history, sociology, politics, and a wide variety of specific social issues that are still relevant today, not the least of which is the Black Lives Matter movement.

Roll of Thunder is a novel rich in the sorts of things English teachers admire: it's a good story well told. It features a rich cast of interesting characters—heroes and villains—who are developed in a variety of ways. The central characters are fully and realistically developed; even the narrator, Cassie, has obvious flaws. Though it is longer than many YA novels, the plot has plenty of tension and surprises that prevent it from bogging down. The suspenseful plot holds readers' interest, and the emotion readers derive from the characters' struggles elevate the book to something more than just a good historical novel.

Taylor's artistry with words lifts the novel even higher. As the following sentence shows, she makes good use of figurative language and specific descriptive detail: "Before us the narrow, sun-splotched road wound like a lazy red serpent dividing the high forest bank of quiet, old trees on the left from the cotton field, forested by giant green and purple stalks on the right" (p. 6). The story is awash with similar memorable—and beautiful—images and turns of phrase.

Though not cluttered by symbolism, *Roll of Thunder* contains symbols for those who search. Perhaps the novel's most famous symbol is the fig tree on the Logans' property. Papa Logan points out that even though the bigger oak and walnut trees overshadow the fig, the smaller tree will survive: "that fig tree's got roots that run deep, and it belongs in that yard as much as the oak and walnut" (Taylor, p. 206). In addition to its aesthetic qualities, *Roll of Thunder* offers many opportunities to discuss thematic concerns of interest to teenagers: family, friendship, alienation, and equality. The following activities are formatted for classroom use.

Because *Roll of Thunder* is so popular, there are many published reading/teaching guides available, for teaching the novel. Many teachers use the book in literature circles; Rebecca Callan has even published a guidebook to the novel, *Literature Circle Guide: Roll of Thunder, Hear My Cry* (2003). A Google search shows that the internet is awash with teaching ideas for Taylor's famous novel. *Roll of Thunder* often appears in English or languages arts classes as part of a multicultural literature unit, but it is also effectively used during Black History Month and, of course, as a free-standing novel.

TEACHING ACTIVITIES

What follows is a range of classroom writing and discussion activities that will help students make text-to-text, text-to-world, and text-to-self connections about *Roll of Thunder, Hear My Cry*, its historical context, and its relationship to contemporary society.

Individual

Text-to-text connections: Read *All American Boys* (Reynolds and Kiely, 2015) and compare Rashad to T. J. Avery. In what ways does their race complicate their lives? How are the roles of white characters similar and different in the two stories? How does each character experience justice? How are their situations similar? How are they different?

Text-to-world connections: Conduct research to learn about the murders of young African Americans in history (e.g., Emmett Till) or more recently (e.g., Trayvon Martin). What parallels can you find between those events and some parts of *Roll of Thunder*? How has racist behavior changed since the 1930s? In what ways might it still be the same?

Range of writing strategies:

1. Taylor describes rain this way: "the tat-tat of the rain against the tin roof changed to a deafening roar that sounded as if thousands of giant rocks were being hurled against the earth" (45). Choose a sound occurring near where you live or go to school—falling rain, a train passing, a rushing river, cars honking, animals making sounds, and so on—and describe the sound in words.
2. Select a passage from *Roll of Thunder* where Taylor describes in detail a bit of Cassie's world. Highlight Taylor's use of figurative language and of specific concrete detail. Now consider a favorite place that you are very familiar with. Using Taylor's passage as your model, write your own description of that place using figurative language and specific, concrete detail.

Small Group

Range of print and nonprint texts: Using digital photos and images from various websites, "African American Odyssey" [http://memory.loc.gov/ammem/aaohtml/aohome.html] and "America from the Great Depression to World War II: Photographs from the FSA-OWI, 1935–1945" [http://www.loc.gov/teachers/classroommaterials/connections/depression-bw/] or other online sources create a collage that represents your favorite scenes from *Roll*

Table 6.1   Terms for Student Investigation

Jim Crow	White Citizens' Councils	Plessy v. Ferguson
The Great Depression	Cotton farming	The Dred Scott Case
The Mississippi Delta	Miscegenation laws	W. E. B. Dubois
Sharecropping	Voter literacy tests	Booker T. Washington
Tenant farming	Lynch laws	Fannie Lou Hamer
Racial segregation	The Natchez Trace	Malcolm X
Reconstruction	Mortgages	Emmett Till
Ku Klux Klan	The New Deal	Slavery
Civilian Conservation	Farm Security	Boycott
Corps	Administration	Cotton gin
Southern Tenant Farmers	Carpetbaggers	Northern Migration
Union	The Scottsboro Boys	

of Thunder. Write a paragraph that explains how the photographs represent the story.

Range of strategies and variety of audiences for different purposes: With a few classmates, plan and write an issue of a local newspaper that could have served Cassie Logan's community. Some "reporters" will conduct historical research that will allow you to write news stories and interviews that reflect the real events and issues of 1933 Mississippi. Other "reporters" can write articles or interviews based on events and characters from *Roll of Thunder*. Work with your classmates to layout your newspaper and post it on a class blog or wiki.

Conduct research on issues and interests: Divide the following terms equally among the members of your group. Conduct research to find an accurate definition of each term, and write it down in your own words. After you have a definition, find a good example of each term that you've defined. Your good example might be anything that helps you or someone who's unfamiliar with the term understand what it means. Photographs, drawings, newspaper articles, or encyclopedia entries are examples of possible good examples of the terms you choose. Share what you've learned with your group, and discuss how these terms relate to *Roll of Thunder* (See table 6.1).

Seven Whole-Class Activities

Here are seven class activities that teachers can use to engage the whole class. Many of them build on the terms that are in table 6.1. Indeed, the small-group activities can function as a lead into what the teachers decides the class might focus on as a group.

1. Have the students create a family tree/pedigree chart that contains all of the Logan characters. Discuss the traits of each character and his/her role in *Roll of Thunder*.

2. What is sharecropping? How did it work and what effect did it have on sharecroppers? Discuss also who the sharecroppers are in *Roll of Thunder* and what their attitudes are toward the system. How was a tenant farmer different from a sharecropper?
3. What is Jim Crow? What were the Black Codes? Find examples of these social policies in American history and in *Roll of Thunder*.
4. What was Reconstruction? How did it affect African Americans in the South? Who was opposed to it? Why were they opposed? What are some things those people did to undermine Reconstruction?
5. Look up information on the following real people: Frederick Douglass, Hiram Revels, Blanche Bruce, Ida B. Wells Barnett, Booker T. Washington, W. E. B. DuBois, Lloyd Gaines, A. Philip Randolph, Emmett Till, Medgar Evers, James Chaney, Linda Brown, Thurgood Marshall, James Meredith, and Fannie Lou Hamer. Why are they important characters in Mississippi and/or African American history? Which of these people might be similar to characters in *Roll of Thunder*?
6. The Fifteenth Amendment and the Civil Rights Act of 1875 were political attempts to provide equality for African Americans. How successful were these attempts? What other political efforts were tried from 1870 to 1940? Which ones had a direct effect on the Logan family or other characters in *Roll of Thunder*?
7. Learn about the 1892 U.S. Supreme Court ruling *Plessy* v. *Ferguson*. How did it reinforce the decision in the 1857 *Dred Scott* case? What effect did *Plessy* v. *Ferguson* have on African Americans in the South? Find examples of the results of that Supreme Court ruling that affected characters in *Roll of Thunder*.

CONCLUSION

Since its publication, *Roll of Thunder, Hear My Cry* has continued to be in print and remained a popular choice in classrooms across the United States. As a result, there are many published reading/teaching guides available for teaching the novel. That can be used in conjunction with the activities described earlier. To begin, many teachers use the book in literature circles; Rebecca Callan has even published a guidebook to the novel, *Literature Circle Guide: Roll of Thunder, Hear My Cry* (2003).

A Google search shows that the Internet is awash with teaching ideas for Taylor's famous novel. *Roll of Thunder* often appears in English or languages arts classes as part of a multicultural literature unit, but it is also effectively used during Black History Month and, of course, as a free-standing novel. In addition, for the many curious readers and students in the classroom, it is an easy step for teachers to remind them that this fine novel is only one book in the continuing saga of the Logan family.

Mildred D. Taylor's Primary Works

Song of the Trees, Puffin (1975)
Roll of Thunder, Hear My Cry, Puffin (1976)
Let the Circle Be Unbroken, Puffin (1981)
The Friendship, Puffin (1987)
The Gold Cadillac, Puffin (1987)
Mississippi Bridge, Puffin (1990)
The Road to Memphis, Puffin (1990)
The Well, Puffin (1995)
The Land, Phyllis Fogelman Books (2001)

RELATED SCHOLARLY WORKS

Barker, Jani L. "Racial Identification and Audience in *Roll of Thunder, Hear My Cry* and *The Watsons Go to Birmingham—1963*." *Children's Literature in Education* 41 (2010): 118–145.

Crowe, Chris. *Teaching the Selected Works of Mildred D. Taylor*. Portsmouth, NH: Heinemann, 2007.

Crowe, Chris. *Presenting Mildred D. Taylor*. New York: Twayne, 1999.

Davis-Undiano, Robert Con. "Mildred D. Taylor and the Art of Making a Difference." *World Literature Today* 78, no. 2 (2004): 11–13.

Hardstaff, Sarah. "'Papa Said That One Day I Would Understand': Examining Child Agency and Character Development in *Roll of Thunder, Hear My Cry* Using Critical Corpus Linguistics." *Children's Literature in Education*. 46 (2015): 226–241.

Harper, Mary Turner. "Merger and Metamorphosis in the Fiction of Mildred D. Taylor." *Children's Literature Association Quarterly* 13, no. 1 (1988): 75–80.

McDonough. "Pathways to Critical Consciousness: A First-Year Teacher's Engagement with Issues of Race and Equity." *Journal of Teacher Education* 60, no. 5 (2009). 528–537.

McDowell, Kelly. "*Roll of Thunder, Hear My Cry*: A Culturally Specific, Subversive Concept of Child Agency." *Children's Literature in Education* 33, no. 3 (2002): 213–225.

Marler, Myrna Dee. Representations of the black male, his family, culture, and community in three writers for African-American young adults:

Mildred D. Taylor, Alice Childress, and Rita Williams-Garcia. PhD diss., University of Hawai'i at Mänoa, August 2001.

Rees, David. "The Color of Skin: Mildred Taylor." *The Marble in the Water.* Boston: Horn Book, 1980. 104–113.

Sims, Rudine. "What Has Happened to the 'All-White' World of Children's Books?" *The Phi Delta Kappan* 64, no. 9 (1983): 650–653.

Smith, Karen Patricia. "A Chronicle of Family Honor: Balancing Rage and Triumph in the Novels of Mildred D. Taylor." *African-American Voices in Young Adult Literature: Tradition, Transition, Transformation.* Metuchen, NJ: Scarecrow, 1994: 247–276.

REFERENCES

Davis-Undiano, Robert Con. "Mildred D. Taylor and the Art of Making a Difference." *World Literature Today* 78, no. 2 (2004): 11–13.

Fritz, Jean. Rev of *Quincy's Harvest* and *Roll of Thunder, Hear My Cry. The New York Times,* November 21, 1976.

Holtze, Sally Holmes. Rev. of *Roll of Thunder, Hear My Cry. The Horn Book Magazine* 52, no. 6 (1976): 627.

Kirkus Reviews (1976). "Roll of thunder, Hear my cry". Retrieved from https://www.kirkusreviews.com/book-reviews/mildred-d-taylor/roll-of-thunder-hear-my-cry/

Larrick, Nancy. "The All-White World of Children's Books." *Saturday Review,* September 11, 1965: 63–65, 84–85.

Myers, Walter Dean. "Children's Books: 'I Actually Thought We Would Revolutionize the Industry.'" *The New York Times,* November 91, 1986."

Myers, Walter Dean. "Where Are the People of Color in Children's Books?" *The New York Times,* March 15, 2014.

Pace Nilsen, Alleen. "A Roundup of Good Books." *English Journal,* September 1977, 84–88.

Rees, David. "The Color of Skin: Mildred Taylor." *The Marble in the Water.* Boston: Horn Book, 1980. 104–113.

Stenson, Leah Deland. Rev of *Roll of Thunder, Hear My Cry. School Library Journal,* September 1976: 140.

Stones, Rosemary. Rev of *Roll of Thunder, Hear My Cry. The Times Literary Supplement,* December 2, 1977: 1415.

Taylor, Mildred D. "ALAN Award Acceptance Speech," ALAN Breakfast, Detroit Michigan, November 22, 1997.

Taylor, Mildred D. "Newbery Medal Acceptance." *The Horn Book Magazine* 53, no. 4 (1977): 401–409.

Taylor, Mildred D. *Roll of Thunder, Hear My Cry,* 40th Anniversary Special Edition. New York: Dial Books for Young Readers, 2016.

Part III

FOUNDING AUTHORS, CURRENT REPUTATIONS, AND THEIR CONTINUED PRESENCE

Chapter 7

Poet of Harlem

The Truth, Text, and Legacy of Walter Dean Myers

M. Cathrene Connery

Standing on the corner of 135th and Malcolm X Boulevard, feet bear witness to a tiny island where the Earth's mightiest rivers—the Congo, Mississippi, Euphrates, and Nile—embrace Manhattan (Conwill, 1988). Here, among the collage of old tenements and new apartment towers, a community of proud, diverse peoples established a homeland for the African diaspora.

Here, within the heat of Silvia's kitchens, the blast of trumpets inside the Cotton Club, and cool velvet of the Apollo Theatre, a unique, American Renaissance was born. Here, children who joyfully splashed in the waters of fire hydrants forged a myriad of rich identities, ideologies, and cultural artifacts of the Black Arts Movement (BAM). Here, in Harlem, and *Here in Harlem* (2004a), lies the truth, text, and legacy of Walter Dean Myers.

TRUTH IN CON-TEXT

A cultural-historical explication of the writer's critical reception requires a causal-genetic analysis of the author's works in con-text (Vygotsky, 1986), for Myers's life and works are tightly enmeshed with the historical-political and social-cultural significance of the world's most famous neighborhood. Once "an ultramodern urban environment for middle and upper-class whites" (Myers, 2001, p. 79), Harlem has evolved into one of the most densely populated areas of the United States.

Located in the heart of New York City, millions of immigrants have claimed the oasis as a second homeland. A complex web of water, cement, and steel veins have long channeled Harlem's guts, grit, and glamour to various parts of the City, as the lifeblood sustaining the Big Apple as a premier economic, cultural, and communications center. Myers' children's books and adolescent novels capture this vibrance for his readers as well as anyone.

Walter Dean Myers was born on August 12, 1937, in Martinsburg, West Virginia, the sixth child in a blended family. His ancestors were enslaved in Virginia during the mid-1800s. After Emancipation, Myers's great-great-uncle relocated his family from a plantation in Leetown to the place of his birth. Myers's biological mother passed away when Walter was three, leaving his father, George, to raise the child and his two stepsisters alone (Myers, 2001).

However, George's former wife, Florence, and her second husband, Herbert Dean, interceded to provide a home for the siblings in their Harlem apartment (Myers, 2001). The young child flourished among the stories, attention, and love he received in his extended, multiracial family, later assuming the pen name "Dean" to honor Florence and Herbert, who raised him (Myers, 2001).

At the end of the nineteenth century, the first waves of the Great Migration reached Harlem as freed people sought lives of safety, agency, and achievement in northern cities and the west. The Deans were one family of almost six million Americans who fled the restricted opportunities, racial segregation, and brutal violence of southern, Jim Crow law between 1915 and 1970 (Wilkerson, 2011).

By the time the Deans relocated to New York, Harlem had become a "majority black neighborhood" known for its vibrant intellectual, artistic, and political activity (Compton, 2017, p. 6). The Harlem Renaissance produced a plethora of African American writers, artists, scholars, and leaders who used their experience, expertise, and talents in multiple mediums to present the dignity of the African diaspora and African American cultures. Mitchell (1994) ascribes that the literary dimension of the cultural movement began "around 1919, reached its peak in the years between 1925 and 1929, and tapered off in the late 1930's" (p. 2).

Innovators and scholars of the Harlem Renaissance promoted an ideology emphasizing individuality and self-respect, calling *all* citizens to combat multiple forms of racism. Novelists, poets, painters, and playwrights from Alain Locke to Zora Neale Hurston sculpted society by introducing the realities of "alienation, irony, bourgeois values, female sexuality, and urban life into the American consciousness" (Mitchell, ibid.).

While the Harlem Renaissance embodied a highly significant, critical, and proud period of self-exploration and community development, Compton (2017) warns against romanticizing the movement, noting the vast majority of the neighborhood's residents—like the Deans—struggled due to the overcrowding, poor sanitation, unemployment, and racial tension produced by European-American economic colonialism (p. 4).

The same social forces prevented the widespread publication and exhibition of its creative products. Tragically, Myers would not hear of—nor read or receive formal instruction in—the master works of the Harlem Renaissance until almost thirty years after he attended public school (Myers, 2001).

The Great Depression of the 1930s brought an end to the Harlem Renaissance, resulting in an era of great hardship. The residents of Harlem, and African American communities across the nation, disproportionately endured discrimination, unemployment, under-employment, dispossession, starvation, homelessness, and violence. An ideological shift occurred as a result of the dialectic between the suffering and resilience of individuals, emphasizing human dignity within the collective experience (Reitano, 2018).

As families struggled to survive, African American intellectuals in Harlem assumed leadership roles (Reitano, 2018) while "creative writers . . . set the stage for an African-American school of protest fiction and humanistic/ ethical criticism," moving from the work of Langston Hughes to Richard Wright's *Native Son* (Mitchell, 1994, p. 6).

As a child within this historical-political, sociocultural context during the 1940s, Myers asserted, "I am the product of Harlem, and of the values, color, toughness, and caring I found there as a child. . . . I learned my flat jump in the church basement and got my first kiss during recess at Bible school. I played the endless street games kids played in the pre-television days and paid enough attention to candy and junk food to dutifully alarm my mother" (Drew, 1994, p. 289). Florence read magazines and comics to the boy, cultivating the boy's connections with books and a vibrant imagination (Myers, 2001).

An early reader, Myers described the reading process as a transaction with text (Rosenblatt, 1994) in which "every book was a landscape on which I was free to wander" (Myers, 2014, p. 1). Delighted by the discovery of the free, public library as a third space (Elmborg, 2011) and "treasured place," the young boy immersed himself in reading literature, and "was tough enough to carry the books home through the streets without too many incidents" (Drew, 1994, p. 290).

However, racist symbols and demeaning characters in the books made a harmful imprint on Myers's growing identity. He later explained the overt, uncontested publication of prejudiced subject matter for mixed-race, intergenerational audiences to be pernicious, affirming, "I had already internalized the negative images, had taken them for truth . . . books were important, and yet it was in books that I found . . . blacks who were lazy, dirty, and above all, comical" (Drew, 1994, p. 291).

In elementary school, Myers first began to write poems that ingeniously avoided words and sounds difficult to pronounce due to a speech impediment.

He credited the encouragement of his 4th-grade teacher with forging his love for reading, inner speech (Ehrich, 2006), and a lifelong exploration of written language (Atkins-Goodson, 2008), explaining, "Writing . . . was a way to overcome the hindrance of speech problems as I tried to reach out to the world. It was a way of establishing my humanity in a world that often ignores the humanity of those in less favored positions" (Drew, 1994, p. 289).

As Myers came of age during the early 1950s, the adolescent witnessed the integration of major league baseball, the military, and public school education. Reading and sports provided personal sources of achievement, refuge, and catharsis from the stresses of school, poverty, and racism, including violence from gangs, depression, alcoholism, addiction, and the murder of close family members.

While the youth experienced an intense hunger for books during this time, Myers felt disconnected with the subject matter available, noting, "As I discovered who I was, a black teenager in a white-dominated world, I saw that these characters, these lives, were not mine. . . . What I wanted, needed really, was to become an integral and valued part of the mosaic that I saw around me" (Myers, 2014, p. 1).

With the encouragement of a caring English teacher, Myers began to compose poetry in composition notebooks, emulating British poets. The intelligent student discovered he enjoyed the mental and linguistic challenges of writing. Yet, the literary landscapes on which the youth wandered left him feeling estranged from his family, friends, and life in Harlem. The teen wondered, "Where and how I would fit into a society that basically didn't like me" (Myers, 2001, p. 113). As the end of school approached, the adolescent became truant, fearing a future he could not imagine or reference in daily life.

One day, while waiting in the principal's office for his mother, the same teacher walked in and inquired if he was in trouble, whispering, "Whatever happens . . . don't stop writing" (Myers, 2001, p. 153). After a few unsuccessful home-school interventions, Myers ended up dropping out of school altogether.

TRUTH IN TEXT

Myers enlisted in the US Army as a radio technician, joining the larger corpus of African American military personnel who dedicated their talents and lives during the Vietnam War. After serving and dying in larger numbers than their European American comrades, veterans of color returned home to the ongoing cultural war that denied their contributions and equal rights as African Americans.

Back in Harlem, Myers found employment as a post office worker, a construction worker, and in a host of other jobs, until the memory of his English teacher's words, suddenly struck him one day (Myers, 2001). He returned to writing.

However, Myers's literary homecoming did not occur until he read Langston Hughes's (1952) *Laughing to Keep from Crying* "at a point in my life when I thought all writers were white, and the subject of any book had to be far removed from my own experiences. . . . Hughes had treated the black experience with a style and dignity which I had felt" (Drew, 1994, p. 290).

James Baldwin's (1957) *Sonny's Blues* also resonated with the author "for it took place in Harlem. . . . By humanizing the people who were like me, Baldwin's story also humanized me. The story gave me a permission I didn't know I needed, the permission to write about my own landscape, my own map" (Myers, 2014, p. 2).

Additionally inspired by the Civil Rights Movement, Myers sought out Baldwin to discover the shared experience of having to leave Harlem to come into their own selves as African American individuals, family members, citizens, and writers (Myers, 2004).

The encounter catapulted the young man to return to his writing at a time when progressive art forms hallmarked the 1960s and 1970s (Frederick, 2016, p. 1). As the birthplace of the BAM, Harlem's many residents "were adamant in their aim to reveal the particularities—struggles, strengths, and celebrations of African-Americans through the creation of poetry, novels, visual art, and theater" (Frederick, 2016, p. 1).

In keeping with BAM's literary heritage, Myers took his own place in the long line of Harlem's talented artists and thinkers, capturing the integrity of his home community in juvenile literature. Grateful for Baldwin's mentoring, Myers later lamented, "How much more meaningful it would have been to have known Baldwin's story at 15, or at 14. Perhaps even younger, before I had started my subconscious quest for identify" (Myers, 2014, p. 2).

In 1969, when the author formally entered the publishing industry, the field of children's literature did not represent youth of color or children coming of age in economically vulnerable communities (Myers, 2014, p. 2). His first novel, *Fast Sam, Cool Clyde, and Stuff* (1975), introduced readers to Harlem through the eyes of an African American protagonist new to the neighborhood.

Myers went on to craft a hybrid of sub-genres for adolescent readers, portraying everyday individual and social dilemmas and celebrated African American heroes, focusing on friendship, love, family, and community. A poet at heart (*Jazz*, 2006) whose mastery of genre eclipsed humor, mystery, and one-act plays, the author is best known for his honest, positive, and hopeful portrayal of urban youth, coming of age within challenging and, sometimes, dangerous circumstances.

Myers's talents in rendering character, voice, and action introduce readers to fellow problem solvers and peer role models also engaged in the quest to achieve independence, belonging, dignity, agency, and integrity.

Targeting the developmental themes faced by teenagers from marginalized and economically vulnerable communities, his protagonists and audiences co-navigate predicaments across contemporary realistic fiction in sports stories (*Hoops*, 1983; *Slam!* 1996; *Game*, 2008a); romance (*What They Found: Love on 145th Street*, 2007; *Carmen*, 2011; addiction (*Dope Sick*, 2009); gangs and crime (*Scorpions*, 1988b; *Shooter*, 2004b); the judicial system, detention, and prison (*Somewhere in the Darkness*, 1992; *Lockdown*, 2010); race (*Monster*, 1999b); and war (*Fallen Angels*, 1988a; *Sunrise over Fallujah*, 2008b).

Myers's use of primary journals as a source and sub-genre in his historical fiction distinguish both his research process and creative production, noted in titles including: *The Journal of Scott Pendleton Collins: A World War II soldier* (1999b) and *The Journal of Joshua Loper: A Black Cowboy* (1999c).

A survey of his biographies and information books, such as *Malcolm X: By Any Means Necessary* (1993); *At Her Majesty's Request: An African Princess in Victorian England* (1999a); and *Now Is Your Time!: The African-American Struggle for Freedom* (1991), represents some of the earliest, albeit limited, efforts of children's publishers to portray African American history.

More recently, the breadth and depth of Myers's artistry is displayed in the futuristic, urban drama *On a Clear Day* (2014a), located at one end of the literary continuum, while the information text *Just Write: Here's How!* (2012) sits at the other.

Early in his career, Myers asserted, "Ultimately, what I want to do with my writing is make the connection—reach out and touch the lives of my characters and share them with a reader" (Drew, 1994, p. 291). In time, his goals more completely validated the power of his art, observing, "Books transmit values. They explore our common humanity" (Myers, 2014, p. 2).

Noting the failure of modern media and the book publishing industry to move beyond the representation of "blacks as victims," Myers challenged the social construction of race probing, "Where are white people going to get their ideas and knowledge of people of color? Where are black children going to get a sense of who they are and what they can be?" (Myers, 2014, p. 3).

His personal answer was to pen a plethora of award-winning texts, including the intimate assemblage of poetry, *Here in Harlem: Poems in Many Voices* (2004). The collection stands as a seminal work in the tradition of the BAM; a cross-analysis of its linguistic sketches reveals Myers's roots and various leitmotifs embedded within his many titles.

Published by Holiday House in 2004, *Here in Harlem* originated when the author first read Edgar Lee Master's (1915) *Spoon River Anthology* in high school during the 1940s. Drawing on Master's example, Myers (2004) shared, "The idea of creating a fictional town and people . . . intrigued me. As the idea for this book ripened in my mind, I began to imagine a street corner in Harlem, the Harlem of my youth, and the very much alive people who would pass that corner" (p. viii).

In contrast to Master's fictional account, Myers's characters represented "people I have known or whose lives touched mine" including heroes, "who sweat from day to day just to survive" and "pictures of scenes for inner-city youth that are familiar . . . scenes with brothers and aunts and friends they all have met" (Myers, 2014, p. viii).

On the cover of the book, a brown-and-white photograph of a handsome Duke Ellington, flanked by stylish back-up singers from 1938, welcomes adolescents to accompany them down a street back in time. The table of contents provides a menu including an introduction by the author; the six testimonies of a focal character who unifies the larger collection; and fifty-three separate poems titled by the name, age, and occupation of a resident of Harlem the reader will meet on the urban landscape.

Sepia photographs and graphic reproductions from the author's personal collection are interspersed among the poems. Dated between 1900 and 1980, baby pictures, street scenes, event posters, wedding portraits, and record labels capture "the sainted, weak ones, and the strong" on their way to church, hard at work, or otherwise engaged in the creation of art, history, and culture in the everyday and traditional celebrations of their lives. The visual text lets readers time-travel through the author's wise, informed, and loving eyes "in a sustained triumph of place and community" (Myers, 2014, p. viii).

The poetic record is divided into five sections by the testimony of Ms. Clara Brown. Written in short, direct, and vivid prose, Ms. Clara's conversational snippets establish the structure of the text, authority of the residents, and circle of community; her warm, confidential, and affable tone requires readers to assume the stance of a neighbor or witness.

Ms. Clara's insights and experience of eighty-seven years also serve as a literary touchstone from which Myers navigates and returns his audience. Readers stray from Ms. Clara's communal corner to venture past pedestrians, cross intersections, and walk city blocks, passing in and out of brownstones and storefront churches into the minds, hearts, and lives of Harlem's residents.

The voices of students and retirees, laborers and artists, veterans and clergy, business people and medical personnel are related in a written collage of neighbors between the ages of twelve and eighty-two. The authentic, elegant, and emotional rendering with which Myers expertly crafted each of the fifty-three poems relays the beauty, intelligence, and tenacity of Harlem's residents in portraits of human dignity residing on a geography of strength, struggle, and hope. The book culminates with a brief account of significant personages, locations, and vocabulary central to the history of the neighborhood.

Pinède's (2004) meticulous review of *Here in Harlem* affirmed the historical and literary merits of the work, vetting Myers's truth to text. Applauding his goal to capture the "vital community as one that is very special to a lot of people," she confirmed the success and faithfulness of his goal to present his neighbors "as richly endowed with those universal traits of love, humor, and ambition as any in the world" (Pinède, 2004, p. 60).

By the end of his life, Myers's dedication to inner city youth coming up in economically vulnerable circumstances affirmed his commitment "to make them human in the eyes of readers, and, especially, in their own eyes. I need to make them feel as if they are a part of America's dream, that all the rhetoric is meant for them, and that they are wanted in this country" (Myers, 2014b, p. 2–3).

In recreating his own epiphany with Baldwin, *Here in Harlem* (2004) moves beyond the cityscape of Myers's youth to the construction of a catharsis in which his readers are "struck by the recognition of themselves in the story, a validation of their existence as human beings, an acknowledgement of their value by someone who understands who they are" (2014, p. 2).

TRUTH IN LEGACY

The pedagogical possibilities for implementing *Here in Harlem* (2004) in the secondary classroom are infinite. As a mentor text, language arts teachers can point to Myers's craft of intentional vocabulary, whispering verse, and intertwining narratives; social studies educators can highlight the writer's historical detail, insider's perspective, and salient themes of place and period.

Braiding a cultural-historical approach to creative education (CHACE) (Connery & John-Steiner, 2012; Connery, John-Steiner, & Marjanovic-Shane, 2018), interdisciplinary conyent study, and critical literacy (Shor, 1999), practitioners can address the robust themes and standards of the National Council for the Social Studies (NCSS, 2010) including, "people, places, and environments," "individual development and identity," or "time, continuity, and change."

Educators can also utilize the mentor text to develop their students' literacy proficiencies outlined in the National Council of Teachers of English and International Literacy Association's Standards for the English Language Arts (2012). While *Here in Harlem* (2004) lends itself to enhancing meaning makers' competencies across all twelve standards, the seventh standard particularly provides a venue by which practitioners can motivate and empower a class community, while polishing the rich talents and challenges of *all* students, through the individual, small-group, whole-group instruction:

> Students conduct research on issues and interests by generating ideas and questions, and by posing problems. They gather, evaluate, and synthesize data from a variety of sources (e.g., print and non-print texts, artifacts, people) to communicate their discoveries in ways that suit their purpose and audience. (NCTE/ILA, 2012)

Toward this end, the following pedagogical sequence seeks to engage, empower, and enrich learners and their neighborhoods within a dynamic, multimodal readers' and writers' workshop.

Engaging with *Here in Harlem*

During the prereading phase, teachers can engage their students by introducing the author as an example of agency, authenticity, and intention. In keeping with research on the development of adolescents, artists, and inventors (John-Steiner, 1985; Vygotsky, 1991), teachers can establish Myers as a "distant mentor" whose richly documented coming of age, creative processes, and commitments can directly parallel or inspire their students.

While reading *Here in Harlem* (2004), thinkers can explore reflections of the "key social, economic and cultural characteristics" to "expand their knowledge of diverse peoples and places" through the multiplicity of Myers's voiced portraits (NCSS, 2010, p. 3–4). Teachers can mindfully design and guide conversations for individual, small-, and whole-group contexts to examine "language use that questions the social construction of the self" (Shor, 1999, p. 2).

During the postreading phase, students can consider the historical-political, sociocultural context of the author's childhood to identify the dialectic between time, place, and people, drawing on Myers's comment, "That space of earth was no ghetto; it was home. Those were not exotic stereotypes; those were my people. And I love them" (Pinède, 2004, p. 60). By pointing out how Myers adopted a transformative activist stance (Stetsenko, 2016) to his life and art, teachers can invite students to touch their futures, community, and society.

Empowering with *Here in Harlem*

Teachers can then encourage meaning makers to empower themselves by scrutinizing their "ongoing development, to reveal the subjective positions from which we make sense of the world and act in it" (Shor, p. 2). During this prewriting phase, youth can generate a list of questions regarding their own personal histories and home. By actively inquiring into their own lives and communities to answer their inquiries, adolescents can develop content knowledge, digital skills, and language arts proficiencies through a critical analysis of their place within their own communities.

Drawing on Myers's own creative process, students can bring in past and current photos "to write poems about them, and what their lives would be like. . . . They can write about the things that they see. Make a list of people in your neighborhood and create a poem about how they were feeling that day, or about a particular event" (Williams, 2005, p. 1). Standing on the shoulders of Baldwin and Myers, teenagers can be invited to critically reflect on and creatively construct their lives.

Teachers can draw on Myers's method as an artist-in-residence, challenging students to "write a certain amount of lines. . . . Write a poem with rhymes in the middle of the sentence instead of the end" to change "the way they approach language" having "heard a rapper do that" (Williams, 2005, p. 1). When provided the opportunity to imagine and examine the past, connect with and communicate the present, youth can and will empower themselves to envision and actualize the future.

Enriching with *Here in Harlem*

Finally, students can enrich others by creating and sharing cultural artifacts that capture their academic and literary pursuits listed earlier. For example, a class might elect to co-construct their own collection of poetry using *Here in Harlem* as a prototype to interview or read to senior citizens at a local assisted living facility. Students might host a cross-country digital poetry reading conference at their neighborhood library.

Youth might capture their cultures, communities, and creative works in a series of podcasts for StoryCorps' Griot program. Using Myers's elegant example, the economy of poetry can be used to cultivate family members, stakeholders, authorities, and the larger public's understanding of their lived experiences, forthright testimonies, and fierce struggles. By asking our youth to "question the way things are and imagine alternatives . . . the word and the world may meet in history for a dream of social justice" (Shor, 1999, p. 25).

Conclusion

Standing on the corner of 135th and Malcolm X Boulevard, feet bear witness to a proud, vital community, the site and source of an American Renaissance. Here, a boy who joyfully splashed in the waters of fire hydrants forged a rich identity, artistry, and vision to become a poet of the BAM, international author, and American treasure. Here, mothers navigate strollers over cement curbsides, careful to avoid awakening their napping angels. Here, sleepy-eyed, short-legged children hurry in flat-footed races to school. Here, passionate teachers dressed to the nines, and principals in three-inch heels, work sixteen-hour days to actualize the future of their students. *Here in Harlem* (2004), and here, in Harlem—and millions of other neighborhoods where youth capture their histories, lives, and futures in print—lies the truth, text, and legacy of Walter Dean Myers.

The author would like to thank Dr. Violet Harris, Ms. Tonya White, and the children, staff, and faculty of the Harlem Children's Zone, whose mentoring informed the writing of this chapter.

REFERENCES

Atkins-Goodson, L. (2008). Walter Dean Meyers: A monster of a voice for young adults. *The Alan Review*, Fall, 26–31.

Baldwin, J. (1957). Sonny's blues. In J. Baldwin, *Going to meet the man*. New York, NY: Vintage.

Compton, A. (2017). *The breath seekers: Race, riots, & public space in Harlem 1900–1935*. New York, NY: City University of New York Academic Works.

Connery, M. C., & John-Steiner, V. (2012). The power of imagination: a cultural-historical approach to creative education. *LEARNing Landscapes, 6*(1), 129–154.

Connery, M. C., John-Steiner, V., & Marjanovic-Shane, A. (2018). *Vygotsky and creativity: A cultural-historical approach to play, meaning making, and the arts*. (2nd ed.). New York: Peter Lang Publishers.

Conwill, H. (1988). Rivers cosmogram [Sculpture mosaic]. Harlem, NY: Schomberg Center for Research in Black Culture.

Drew, Bernard A. (1997). *The 100 most popular young adult authors: biographical sketches and bibliographies*. Englewood, CO: Libraries Unlimited.

Ehrich, J. F. (2006). Vygotskyan inner speech and the reading process. *Australian Journal of Educational and Developmental Psychology, 6*, 12–25.

Elmborg, J. (2011). Libraries as the spaces between us: Recognizing and valuing the third space. *American Library Association Reference & User Services Quarterly, 50*(4), 338–350.

Frederick, C. (2016). *On black aesthetics: The black arts movement*. Retrieved from https://www.nypl.org/blog/2016/07/15/black-aesthetics-bam.

Hughes, L. (1952). *Laughing to keep from crying*. New York, NY: Holt Publishing Company.

John-Steiner, V. (1985). *Notebooks of the mind: Explorations of thinking*. Albuquerque, NM: University of New Mexico Press.

Masters, E. L. (1915). *Spoon River anthology*. London: MacMillan.

Myers, W. D. (1975). *Fast Sam, cool Clyde, and Stuff*. New York, NY: Viking Press.

Myers, W. D. (1983). *Hoops*. New York, NY: Delacorte.

Myers, W. D. (1988a). *Fallen angels*. New York, NY: Scholastic.

Myers, W. D. (1988b). *Scorpions*. New York, NY: Harper & Row.

Myers, W. D. (1991). *Now is your time!: The African-American struggle for freedom*. New York, NY: HarperCollins.

Myers, W. D. (1992). *Somewhere in the darkness*. New York, NY: Scholastic.

Myers, W. D. (1993). *Malcolm X: By any means necessary*. New York, NY: Scholastic.

Myers, W. D. (1996). *Slam!* New York, NY: Scholastic.

Myers, W. D. (1997). *Harlem*. New York, NY: Scholastic.

Myers, W. D. (1999a). *At her majesty's request: An African princess in Victorian England*. New York, NY: Scholastic.

Myers, W. D. (1999b). *Monster*. New York, NY: HarperCollins.

Myers, W. D. (1999c). *The journal of Scott Pendleton Collins: A World War II soldier*. New York, NY: Scholastic.

Myers, W. D. (1999d). *The journal of Joshua Loper: A black cowboy*. New York, NY: Scholastic.

Myers, W. D. (2000). *145th Street: Short stories*. New York, NY: Delacorte.

Myers, W. D. (2001). *Bad boy: A memoir*. New York: Harper-Collins Publishers.

Myers, W. D. (2004a). *Here in Harlem: Poems in many voices*. New York, NY: Holiday House.

Myers, W. D. (2004b). *Shooter*. New York, NY: HarperCollins.

Myers, W. D. (2006). *Jazz*. New York, NY: Holiday House.

Myers, W. D. (2007). *What they found: Love on 145th Street*. New York, NY: Random House.

Myers, W. D. (2008a). *Game*. New York, NY: HarperCollins.

Myers, W. D. (2008b). *Sunrise over Fallujah*. New York, NY: Scholastic.

Myers, W. D. (2009). *Dope sick*. New York, NY: HarperCollins.

Myers, W. D. (2010). *Lockdown*. New York, NY: HarperCollins.

Myers, W. D. (2011). *Carmen*. New York, NY: EdgemontUSA.

Myers, W. D. (2012). *Just write: Here's how!* New York, NY: Harper Collins.

Myers, W. D. (2014a). *On a clear day*. New York, NY: Crown Books for Young Readers.

Myers, W. D. (2014b). Where are the people of color in children's books? *New York Times*. Retrieved from http://www.nytimes.com/2014/03/16/opinion/sunday/where-are-the-people-of-color-in-childrens-books.html?hp&rref=opinion&_r=1

Mitchell, A. (Ed.) (1994). *Within the circle: an anthology of African-American literary criticism from the Harlem Renaissance to the present*. London: Duke University Press.

National Council for the Social Studies. (2017). College, career, and civic life (C3) framework for Social Studies state standards: Guidance for enhancing the rigor of K-12 civics, economics, geography, and history. Retrieved from https://www.socialstudies.org/c3

Pinède, N. (2006). Critical essay [Review of the book *Here in Harlem*]. *Literary Newsmakers for Students, (1),* 46–61.

Reitano, J. (2018). *The restless city: A short history of New York from colonial times to the present*. (3rd ed.). New York: Routledge, Taylor, & Francis.

Rodgers, R. (2002). That's what you're here for, you're suppose to tell us: Teaching and learning critical literacy. *Journal of Adolescent & Adult Literacy, 45*(8), 772–787.

Rosenblatt, L. (1994). *The reader, the text, the poem: The transactional theory of the literary work.* Carbondale, IL: Southern Illinois University Press.

Shor, I. (1999). What is critical literacy? *Journal of Pedagogy, Pluralism and Practice.* 1(4). Retrieved from https://digitalcommons.lesley.edu/jppp/vol1/iss4/2.

Sims, R. (1982). *Shadow and substance: Afro-American experience in contemporary children's fiction.* Urbana, IL: National Council of Teachers of English.

Stetsenko, A. (2016). *The transformative mind: Expanding Vygotsky's perspective on development and education.* New York, NY: Cambridge University Press.

Vygotsky, L. S. (1962; 1986). *Thought and language.* Cambridge, MA: Massachusetts Institute of Technology Press.

Vygotsky, L. S. (1991). Imagination and creativity in the adolescent. *Soviet Psychology, 29,* 1, 73–88, doi: 10.2753/RPO1061–0405290173

Wilkerson, I. (2010). *The warmth of other suns: The epic story of America's great migration.* New York: Vintage Press.

Williams, J. (2005, February 16). A poetic look at Harlem. *New York Post.*

Chapter 8

Reading, Learning, and Telling Folklore through Virginia Hamilton's *Zeely*

Nancy D. Tolson

In 1967, Dr. Martin Luther King, Jr. gives his famous speech "Beyond Vietnam; A Time to Break the Silence," Detroit is set ablaze for five days due to the civil unrest between blacks and police officers, and it is the year before James Brown and bandleader Alfred "Pee Wee" Ellis record the infamous song "Say It Loud, I'm Black and I'm Proud" (1968). A young author by the name of Virginia Hamilton has her first book, *Zeely*, published in 1967 (Hamilton & Shimin, 1967).

Zeely is a children's book that reflects a summer adventure of a brother and sister visiting their uncle who lives on a farm. This junior novel has no racial conflict; it is not influenced by the white presence because there are none, yet this book celebrates the beauty and adoration of a young woman that resembles an African queen from Rwanda. And so Virginia Hamilton created a story that spoke softly that she was black and she was proud.

On the train to their uncle's house, Elizabeth decided to change her name to Geeder and her brother's, John Perry, name to Toe Boy. The two learned to entertain themselves throughout the summer. They roamed the farm and glanced at the stars at night. Geeder discovered that the pig farmer's daughter who was renting land from her uncle's land strongly resembled a Watutsi African queen.

Mr. Tayber and his daughter raise pigs, but there is something else that fascinates Geeder beyond raising pigs in a pig farm. The pigs follow and obey the farmer's daughter, Zeely, like they were her pets. Geeder discovers a picture in a magazine of a Watsutsi queen; a queen who looks remarkably like her neighbor. Geeder now has a new adventure—following Zeely to get to the truth.

Zeely Tayber was more than six and a half feet tall, thin and deeply dark as a pole of Ceylon ebony. She wore a long smock that reached to her ankles. Her arms, hands, and feet were bare, and her thin, oblong head didn't seem to fit quite right on her shoulders. She had very high cheekbones and her eyes seemed to turn inward on themselves. Geeder couldn't say what expression she saw on Zeely's face. She knew only that it was calm, that it had pride in it, and that the face was the most beautiful she had ever seen. (Hamilton, p. 42)

Virginia Hamilton like, folklorist and author Zora Neale Hurston, mixed within her novels folklore and African references. Her stories are enriched with the Black Aesthetic and other cultural evidence that are embodied in the black children within the novel. Hamilton was a storyteller. She created cultural stories that young readers can still enjoy and characters resonate with these readers. Hamilton states, "We want our heritages and our contributions to society to be seen as significant contributions to the social order" (p.71).

Virginia Hamilton was an advocate for the library. She recalled as a child how wonderful library visits were because of the stories told by the Story Lady and as she got older she discovered and read great books. She states, "I have used the public library as a child reader, as a student, as a researcher, and finally, as a writer-turned-lecturer on the subject of my books and writing" (p. 70).

She saw the library as a place where children could hear librarians tell wonderful stories that could eventually be found inside of books they were able to take home. She enjoyed hearing stories told by the Story Lady, a person she believed was partly responsible for her love of reading. This is because this librarian, this storyteller, like her mother, "was the giver of learning. She gave it out freely" (p. 69).

Virginia Hamilton's contribution to the world was an abundance of books filled with tales of adventure like the ones that were told to her as a child by her mother and the librarians. In Hamilton's first book, *Zeely* (1967), she weaved, inside this coming-of-age novel, a folktale and an antidotal tale told by Zeely as a way to persuade Geeder that she was not someone to idolize. Zeely wanted Geeder to see that she was nothing special. Zeely tells Geeder about the old woman that lived near the lake when Zeely lived in Canada.

Zeely liked to swim in the lake and the old woman would scream to her that she was able to see her. Zeely would scream back and "I see you!" (p. 110). One night, Zeely had just finished swimming when the old woman came out. Zeely crept between the bushes and the trees to hide. The old woman kicked a stone, but it wasn't a stone but a turtle that slowly moved into the water. The old woman tapped on a vine that was near Zeely but it wasn't a vine but rather a snake.

The old woman caught Zeely that night but quickly let her go. Because of Zeely's dark skin, the woman thought of her as the night. She literally believed that she had been able to catch the night when she caught Zeely and that made the old woman happy. She was not a queen like Geeder believed but to the old woman, Zeely was the dark night.

STORYTELLING FESTIVAL

Individual Activity

An educator will use *Zeely* as the foundation to create a classroom storytelling festival with the help of several folktale collections by Virginia Hamilton. The teacher will use the two stories Zeely told Geeder while introducing additional tales found in Hamilton's folktale collections.

The teacher will first read aloud Zeely's experience with the old woman at the lake to the class (Hamilton, 1967, pp. 110–112). Another option is for the teacher to read aloud (or memorize and perform) the "Good Blanche, Bad Rose, and the Talking Eggs" found in *Her Stories: African American Folktales, Fairy Tales, and True Tales* (1995). Modeling this form of storytelling illustrates for the students what they will be required to do.

For each story, it is imperative that the teacher knows the story and is able to convey the intended spirit of the characters, tone/mood, and plot of the stories. The scholarship of Jesse S. Gainer and Nancy Valdez-Gainer in their article "Re-Visioning through Storytelling and Story acting in a Second-grade Classroom" posits that the storytelling element will "create a shared world where students and teachers can connect across differences to enact a dialogic curriculum" (p. 101).

Once both stories have been told, ask the students how the old woman that Zeely met while swimming compares to the old woman that Good Blanche met. Move slowly away from the topic of Zeely and into the story "Good Blanche, Bad Rose, and the Talking Eggs." Create a chart that compares and contrasts Blanche and Rose and the eggs and the old woman. How are they alike? How are they different? Additional guiding questions include: How were manners important in these stories? What was the most important moment in each story? Explain why this particular moment is crucial.

Ellin Green states in *Storytelling Art and Technique*, "All children, whether or not they are readers, like to hear a good story told well. After they have heard it, book-loving children want to read it again for themselves" (Green & Del Negro, 2010). Storytelling assists children to formulate images from the words that the storyteller uses to create the story. They use their imagination to color the collection of images they present for their listeners. In other words, the strong and effective storytelling enables students to visualize and make intellectual and emotional connections to the stories.

The teacher should model storytelling for the students; showing them the difference between good Blanche and bad Rose through voice and expression. Guiding questions for the post-reading discussion: How do you think the mother of the two should act? Should speak? Should she change what she is doing? If so, how?

When telling the story, as the teacher, move around the classroom to inform the students that they too may be able to do this when it is their time to tell a story. It is important to create a storytelling atmosphere for the students. When telling the story, freely moving around the room will excite the children and keep them quite attentive. Be mindful to use the body as much as the voice.

If needed, physically involve the audience with the story. Note: when doing a physical tale, make sure to pace the performance. It is important to be aware of how the story is unfolding. The performer does not want to be out of breath and cause the audience to miss any of the details of the tale. Clearly, practicing alone, before family members, or in small groups will help students master this activity.

Ellin Green and Janice Del Negro created the "Reach for a Story" Project, which has ten goals that fit perfectly with this project.

1. To introduce children to the art of storytelling for their own enjoyment and for the entertainment of others.
2. To motivate children to read and to use the resources of the library.
3. To nurture the child's creative imagination.
4. To increase the child's communication skills—listening, speaking, reading and writing.
5. To introduce children to folk literature and modern imaginative stories.
6. To guide children to the selection of tellable tales.
7. To teach children the techniques of learning to tell stories.
8. To build in children their appreciation of cultural differences and similarities.
9. To encourage parents, teachers, librarians, and other professionals to use storytelling in their work with children.
10. To increase the visibility of the library and it program for children. (p. 204)

SMALL-GROUP ACTIVITY

This small-group activity is a classroom storytelling festival. The teacher or students will create small groups. Ideally, all of the groups will be the same size. Each group of students will be given a copy of one of the following of Virginia Hamilton's books: *The People Could Fly* (1985), *Her Stories* (1995), or *A Ring of Tricksters* (1997). (Be sure to have multiple copies of each book if the class is large.)

The students in the groups must select one story to perform for the storytelling festival. The teacher will assist in preventing duplicate stories by dividing the book or assigning a particular story. If two groups want to perform the same story, then the teacher must highlight the fact that each group will have a unique way of performing their story.

Once the students have selected their stories, they will be ready to begin practicing the story. Allow them time in various spaces in the classroom to rehearse lines and movements. As the teacher monitor, give advice, and encourage the students. This project should take no more than two weeks from start to completion. Each day they should have a certain amount of time to work on their project with their group.

Visual artwork is also a part of this classroom storytelling festival. Have the students create individual art pieces that correlate with the story that they will be telling. This exercise allows students to show as well as tell. The interpretations of the stories come alive through the imagination of the child and the art work they produce.

Each group will be given a guide on preparing their story. This guide serves as a checklist for their performance.

The tellers must know the story thoroughly
The tellers projected the story well
The story was interesting
The tellers were exciting

To be truly successful, every member of the group should participate in the performance or visual representation. Given careful planning, good modeling, and vigilant monitoring of student activities, the storytelling at the individual and group levels can be both educational and engaging for the students

WHOLE-CLASS ACTIVITY

Return back to *Zeely* to discuss with the class why Geeder believed Zeely to be a Watutsi queen. Geeder found "a photograph of an African woman of royal birth" (Hamilton, 1967, p. 48). Geeder created an entire story from a photograph. Zeely becomes a queen. With her rich imagination, Geeder convinced herself that Zeely was a Watutsi queen from one photograph. Ironically, Symeon Shimin, the illustrator for *Zeely*, used images he found of the Watutsi Princess Emma Bakayishonga, the daughter of King Mwami Yuhi wa V Musinga of Rwanda in the 1940s, as the physical model for Zeely.

Gather images showing people and places from around the world. Use PowerPoint or an overhead projector so that the entire class can see the variety of images you collect. You might also consider placing all of the images with references on a class webpage so that students can reference them more than once. These images can be used as excellent writing prompts. What treasures of stories can the students create? Writing imaginative stories enables children to pull out the tools needed to formulate the "Four Cs"— critical thinking, communication, collaboration, and creativity (National Education Association, 2019).

CONCLUSION

Virginia Hamilton cherished storytelling and folklore. Her ability to place it in a story such as *Zeely* demonstrates her awareness that adolescents love storytelling too. Storytelling can teach powerful lessons that are remembered longer. One of the most precious treasures that a child possesses is imagination. The activities in this chapter help them soar, but the real inspiration is the vast collection of books that Hamilton has created, of which *Zeely* is prime example.

Geeder is a wonderful character with imagination and creativity. Her characteristics are a model for students. She created an impressive story just from a photograph. Zeely knew that Geeder's imagination was soaring and so she told the tale of the incident at the lake. The tale becomes a source of inspiration for Geeder; the lessons are metaphors that Geeder carries with her "'Remember the turtle,' she murmured, 'remember the snake'" (p. 122). Folklore and storytelling are tools that are always great additions to a teacher's toolbox.

List of Virginia Hamilton's Primary Works

Zeely (1967)
The House of Dies Drear (1968)
The Time-Ago Tales of Jadhu (1968)
The Planet of Junior Brown (1971)
M.C. Higgins the Great (1974)
Paul Robeson: The Life and Times of a Free Black Man (1974)
The Writings of W. E. B. Du Bois (1975)
Arbilla Sun Down (1975)
Justice and Her Brothers (1978)
Dustland (1980)
Jadhu (1980)
The Gathering (1981)
Sweet Whispers, Brother Rush (1982)
Willie Bea and the Time the Martians Landed (1983)

The Magical Adventures of Pretty Pearl (1983)
A Little Love (1984)
The People Could Fly (1985)
Junius over Far (1985)
A White Romance (1987)
The Mystery of Drear House (1987)
Anthony Burns: The Defeat and Triumph of a Fugitive Slave (1988)
In the Beginning: Creation Stories Around the World (1988)
The Bells of Christmas (1989)
Cousins (1990)
The Dark Way: Stories from the Spirit World (1990)
The All Jadhu Storybook (1991)
Drylongso (1992)
Many Thousand Gone (1993)
Plain City (1993)
Her Stories: African American Folktales, Fairy Tales, and True Tales (1995)
Jagarundi (1995)
When Birds Could Talk and Bats Could Sing: The Adventures of Bruh Spar-
    row, Sis Wren, and Their Friends (1996)
A Ring of Tricksters: Animal Tales from America, the West Indies, and Africa
    (1997)
Second Cousins (1998)
Bluish: A Novel (1999)
The Girl Who Spun Gold (2000)
Time Pieces: The Book of times (2001)
Bruh Rabbit and the Tar Baby Girl (2003)
Wee Winny Witch's Skinny: An Original African American Scare Tale (2004)

REFERENCES

Brown, J., & Ellis, A. (1968). "Say it loud—I'm black and I'm proud (Part 1) [Recorded by James Brown]. On say it loud—I'm black and I'm proud [record]. Los Angeles, CA: Vox Studios.

Gainer, J. S., & Valdez-Gainer, N. (2017). Re-visioning through storytelling and story acting in a second-grade classroom (Language Arts Lessons) (Column). *Language Arts, 95*(2), 101–104.

Gillard, M. (1996). *Storyteller, storyteacher: Discovering the power of storytelling for teaching and living.* York, ME: Stenhouse Publishers.

Greene, E., & Del Negro, J. M. (2010). *Storytelling: Art and technique* (4th ed.). Santa Barbara, CA: Libraries Unlimited.

Hamilton, V. (1999). Sentinels in Long Still Rows. *American Libraries, 30*(6), 68–71.
Hamilton, V., & Shimin, S. (1967). *Zeely*. New York,: Macmillan.
National Education Association. (2019). Preparing 21st students for a global society: An educator's guide to the "four Cs." Retrieved from http://www.nea.org/assets/docs/A-Guide-to-Four-Cs.pdf

Chapter 9

Julius Lester's Nonfiction Presentation of Slavery in *To Be a Slave*

Steven T. Bickmore

I was introduced to Julius Lester for the first time shortly after the publication of his outstanding verse novel, Day of Tears. *I was embarrassed that I didn't know any of his earlier work. Slowly, I began reading his children's books and young adult novels. I soon learned he was a major contributor to both fields, as well as a folk singer and photographer who participated in the early events of the Civil Rights Movement.*

The above remembrance is similar to how many current scholars learn about the writings of Julius Lester, as well as many other influential authors. They find one, read it, can't believe they did know him or her earlier and find a treasure trove of quality writing. Lester was a prolific writer. In 1971, he became one of the first professors of African American studies in the United States accepting a job at the University of Massachusetts, Amherst, where he remained until his retirement in 2003.

Many scholars consider Lester to be a major African American contributor in children's literature through his retelling of folk tales and children stories which began in the 1970s and continued into the 2000s. Many of these, if not most, are accompanied by illustrations by some of the era's greatest illustrators of the period, and chief among those is Jerry Pinkey. Nevertheless, the argument remains that two books, *To Be a Slave* (Lester & Feelings, 1968) and *Long Journey Home* (Lester, 1972), establish him as one of the most provocative and influential African American YA authors.

Both books are important deserve the recognition that many other early YA novels receive, like *The Outsiders* (Hinton, 1967), *The Contender* (Lipsyte, 1967), *The Pigman* (Zindel, 1968), *Sounder* (Armstrong, 1969), and *My Darling, My Hamburger* (Zindel, 1969). All of these books are important markers in the history of the genre. Two of these books reflect African American culture. *The Contender* (Lipsyte, 1967) is a realistic picture of a youth finding boxing as survival. *Sounder* (Armstrong, 1969) is historical fiction set during the Depression. Both remain popular and are easily found in libraries. Yet, both are written by cultural outsiders.

At the same time, Julius Lester, an African American, is writing substantial YA nonfiction narratives of the slave experience in America. The first, *To Be a Slave* (Lester & Feelings, 1968), won numerous awards and has been reprinted several times during its first thirty years. The book is an important example of an early "own voice" narrative but hard to find in libraries and not very frequently studied by critics. Yet, early books by cultural outsiders remain accessible.

Simply put, YA literature by African American writers has always been there. Their contributions have been frequently ignored and/or under pro- moted if the topic is historical and/or critical of society's treatment of civil rights issues. If the book is interpreted as capturing a snapshot of inner city life around sports, gangs, or poverty, there is an argument to be made that such texts are promoted. See for example the chapters in this volume on Wal- ter Dean Myers, whose quality works were promoted and highly successful.

Perhaps YA literature written by African American authors served two purposes: one, they draw attention to serious issues that African American youth deal with daily. Second, they reaffirm white readers' assumptions about the plight of the "other" in circumstances they don't experience in the same way. Both are true. One represents an attempt to explore and present reality as experienced. The other, ironically, preserves stereotypes about marginal youth and their communities.

Both reactions remind readers and critics of the reason for this book: To highlight the fact that so few writers, who as insiders within marginalized groups, in this case African American, were published during the first twenty years of the YA classification. And, when they were published, how they were reviewed, critiqued, promoted, interpreted, and remembered. For example, Julius Lester is barely mentioned in the nine editions of *Literature for Today's Young Adults* (Donelson & Nilsen, 1980; Nilsen, Blasingame, Donelson, & Nilsen, 2013) from 1980 to 2013, although the texts are widely seen as foun- dational studies in YA literature.

HOW WE THINK ABOUT JULIUS LESTER NOW

Conducting a Google search on Julius Lester would not necessarily reveal his importance as an African American YA author. Instead, it would disclose a scholar, an African American convert to Judaism, a civil rights advocate, as well as an author of children's and YA literature as well as an author of adult works, religious writings, and historical texts. He is a chameleon, a renaissance man who tells stories, plays the guitar and sings, writes history, discusses religion through writing and practice, and educated students for forty years. Yet, his YA offerings, both early and late, establish him as founding figure focusing on race in America.

To Be a Slave

This chapter highlights Lester's *To Be a Slave* (Lester & Feelings, 1968), a nonfiction account of slave narratives for adolescents crafted primarily from *Born in Slavery: Slave Narratives from the Federal Writers' Project 1936 to 1938* (United States, Works Progress Administration, & Federal Writers' Project, 1937). It is also punctuated by illustrations by Tom Feelings, the first African American to win the Caldecott Honor Award. The book was a 1969 Newbery Honor Book as well as an ALA Notable Book, a School Library Journal's Best Book of the Year, the Smithsonian Best Book of the Year, and was given a 1970 Lewis Carroll Shelf Award.

When most teachers and students think of YA literature, they think of fiction. This is especially true of the early era of YA fiction in the late 1960s when the field was emerging with books like *The Outsiders* (Hinton, 1967), *The Contender* (Lipsyte, 1967), *Mr. and Mrs. Bo Bo Jones* (Head, 1967), *Sounder* (Armstrong, 1969), and *The Chosen* (Potok, 1967).

These books focused on adolescents struggling as they "tried on" adult responsibilities: working, sexual relationships, and taking on the responsibilities of siblings. The struggle with racial tensions, while omnipresent in concerns of inner city struggles, the Vietnam War, and civil rights legislation, was not the thematic focus of most early YA fiction.

In addition, few of the novels written about diverse characters were written by authors who were cultural insiders. For example, both *The Contender* (Lipsyte, 1967) and *Sounder* (Armstrong, 1969*)*, novels that received high praise, were written by cultural outsiders. Granted, it was an era when there was a tighter focus on the novel and not the author. Even less common were nonfiction works written directly for this emerging market. It is notable that in this early period of the YA novel, Lester chose to present a work of nonfiction that focuses on slave narratives. Furthermore, it as a work received numerous accolades.

Lester's text focuses on slave narratives collected during the activities of the Federal Writers' Project 1936–1938 (1937). This is a large collection of recorded and transcribed narrative that were only published in limited ways when Lester began creating his text for younger readers. In total, he draws on three sources. The first influential source B. A. Botkin's *Lay My Burden Down* (1945, 1946) was the initial book from the archives. The second was *The Negro in Virginia* (Writers' Program (Va.), 1940). This was the first, and only, book of a planned collection of state by state "racial studies" finished by the Virginia Writing Project.

The final source was Lester's own study of the archives at the Library of Congress, where he studiously took notes and filed them away. His initial research was inspired by a hope that he might find references about his own ancestors among the recorded slave narratives (Lester & Feelings, 1968, p. 5). But to no avail. He kept reading traditional slave narratives and other sources for several years until he pitched the idea to a children's book editor. Within a few months, the first draft was written and in short order this landmark text, *To Be a Slave*, was published.

The book's style and structure is creative and important, especially in an era that promotes the reading of informational texts. Lester's voice is presented in italics, and the sections that are quoted from the source material are presented in standard format. Such a presentation highlights the voices of the slaves telling their own story. Lester sets aside the power of his own voice and provides minimal editorializing. He carefully ties together each slave's account with skillfully constructed transitions that create a truly rendered "own voices" narrative of the American slave experience.

The book is organized with a prologue and chapters that highlight the major experiences of slaves. There is one chapter each on: To Be a Slave, The Auction Block, and the Plantation. Then two chapters each on Resistance to Slavery and Emancipation. The Prologue provides a context of American slavery beginning in 1619 when slavery was introduced to Jamestown, as Spike Lee stated during his Academy Award acceptance speech (Williams, 2019).

The burden and consequences of American slavery have rarely been adequately taught in the curriculum of American schools. This is lamentable when Julius Lester, a participant in the 1964 Mississippi Summer Project, worked as a photographer for SNCC, and is frequently credited with coining the term "black power" (Ito, 2018). It is noteworthy that this engaged participant, Lester, in the early social justice movement of the 1960s produced a nonfiction account of slavery, written directly for adolescents, that ultimately was unused in either English Language Arts or Social Studies classrooms. The contribution was written but ignored.

In the first chapter, "To Be a Slave," Lester captures the "vicious cruelty. Slaves were whipped for the most trifling incidents" (1968, p. 32). By citing a simple, single statement by Roberta Mason, "They whipped my father 'cause he looked at a slave they killed and cried'" (1968, p. 33). This single moment captures the reality that slaves were, indeed, human and capable of profound empathy. They continued to survive even in the face of continued cruelty.

In each chapter, Lester continues to extract from the archives remarkably stark accounts of each specific moment.

> They would stand the slaves up on the block and talk about what a fine-looking specimen of black manhood or womanhood they was, tell how healthy they was, look in their mouth and examine their teeth just like they was a horse, and talk about the kind of work they would be fit for and could do. Morris Hillyer Library of Congress. (Lester & Feelings, 1968, p. 46)

Lester demonstrates through the slaves' own voices how they were treated and how they tried to reconcile their treatment at the auction block and on the plantation. He also provides a glimpse into how they established their identity through attempts at freedom and after emancipation.

PREREADING: THE PEDAGOGICAL PRACTICES OF VISUAL DISCOVERY

Photographs, drawings, and other images can serve as powerful learning tools, in part because, as John Medina—the author of *Brain Rules*—has observed, the "visual process takes up about half of everything your brain does" (2008, p. 190). The five-step Visual Discovery Strategy (VDS) from Teacher's Curriculum Institute helps adolescents gather and interpret evidence, deconstruct images, and make hypotheses (for a detailed description of VDS, see Hayes, Owens, & Simpson, 2010, pp. 28–37, as well as table 9.1).

The initial two steps of VDS strategy are preparatory. First, the teacher selects an image(s) with powerful visual impact. The most effective images

Table 9.1   Directions for Visual Discovery Strategy (VDS)

Step One	Select powerful images (with layers of meaning) related to the young adolescent literature your students are reading.
Step Two	Project the selected image on a large screen using parliamentary seating, so students are facing each other (in order to facilitate discussion) with a wide aisle in the center leading to the image.
Step Three	Ask carefully sequenced and spiraling questions that lead to discovery. QUESTIONS COULD INCLUDE . . . .
Step Four	Challenge students to read an informational text (a related passage from young adolescent literature reading), which augments the information garnered from an analysis of the image.
Step Five	Have students interact with the images to promote synthesis and demonstrate what they have learned from the visual and textual sources.

Source: Directions for Visual Discovery Strategy (VDS), as described by Lobdell, Owens, & Bower, 2010, pp. 28–37.

offer rich stories or layers of meaning to be unpacked through inspection and analysis. Next, the teacher uses parliamentary seating—half the student desks facing the other half with an aisle in the middle leading to the image. This arrangement promotes discussion and allows students to access the image when needed.

In step three, the teacher guides students through higher levels of thinking about the image through a series of spiraling questions. Carefully scaffold the questions at discrete cognitive levels from gathering evidence, to interpreting the evidence, and finally making hypotheses. This deliberate image analysis models the process that students can employ in their own lives when encountering the array of images that are part of our modern culture.

After analyzing the image, students read an informational text, which augments students' emerging understanding spawned by the image. The supplemental informational text might serve to provide additional details about the image topic. Since this is a before-reading activity, the informational text can provide contexts for the primary text, in this case *To Be a Slave* (Lester & Feelings, 1968). Teacher can select images that are available with free access from the Library of Congress (United States et al., 1937).

In the final step, time permitting, students synthesize information from both the image and the informational text through an Act-It-Out. Student groups step into the image and act out a dialogue, incorporating information from steps three and four. Teachers instruct students to write a short script and/or they might give them role cards. VDS enters students into Wilhelm's evocative dimension "creating mental images and [envisioning] characters, settings, and situations" (2016, p. 87). Encouraging adolescents to consider an image used academically helps them consider the time, context, and issues present in literature or an historical incident.

This practice also helps adolescents gain skills to critically examine the images that confront their lives. In short, VDS is not just an isolated strategy to interest students or introduce informational text, but part of a bigger picture (pun intended) that commits to developing students' long-term literary, historical, and media engagement. The incorporation of VDS encourages more integrated sets of cross-curricular activities and assessments.

DURING READING: STOP AND RESEARCH

The book is built on the Slave Narratives for the Federal Writers Project and it only focuses on one section. In the 1960s, the seventeen volumes in thirty-three parts were not readily available except in the Library of Congress and filed as Slave Narratives: A Folk History of Slavery in the United States from Interviews with Former Slaves (Washington, D.C., 1941). Finally, by 2001, the narratives were digitized and are readily available for free. Now the original 2300 first-person accounts and 500 photographs of former slaves, including 200 that had never been digitized or made public.

There are now seventeen volumes covering seventeen states and all interviews are arranged alphabetically within each state. If a student had the name of an ancestor from one those states it would be an easier matter to see if a narrative from that ancestor existed. In essence, the project could be a genealogical project. Students related to the former slaves could do their genealogy and other students explore the family lines of the slaves' former owner.

For those teachers concerned about the sensitive nature of this inquiry, there is a more practical activity. This activity would not make the research so immediately personal for students related to former slaves, or for students with no immediate or obvious connection to the slaves owners. Teachers would select and prepare for students to read several slave narratives from the archives so that they might create summaries or reports. This could happen in several ways in which student could create individual parts of a collaborative project.

1. Students would find an illustration and the accompanying story and rewrite for a younger audience—elementary or secondary students. This is similar to what Lester did with his narrative. Students would be writing in a similar fashion with similar goals in order to construct a class webpage that would/could be shared with other classes during Black History Month. Each student creates a single illustrated narrative that could provide a day-by-day discussion of slaves lives both during and post their slave experience.
2. A second option is to have students shape the information from a single slave narrative on a single card; thus the members of the class could create a "deck" of cards. The deck becomes a source of quick writing prompts and/or impromptu oral reports where students provide two-minute speeches with accompanying visuals.
3. Similar to creating individual cards, students could create informational posters that could be placed in a gallery of slave narratives that would be put on display in the classroom, the school library, or a public library during Black History Month.

Not only would these activities enhance students' experience with the book, they would create a community response that uses the resources of the Library of Congress and the National Archives.

POSTREADING: WRITING AN INFORMATIVE/
EXPLANATORY TEXT

After studying a nonfiction text, students can be asked to explore and write about topics related to the text studied. For example, several topics that can be connected to slave narratives include the reparations for slavery, the current state of slavery in the world, and abusive labor practices. Anyone of these can provide information that will help students prepare an explanatory essay.

Reparations for slavery in the United States continue to be a topic of discussion among many African American intellectuals, but gain little interest among the general public. Students could analyze several arguments about reparation beginning with a study of the National Coalition of Blacks for Reparations in America (N'COBRA), the success or failure of the "forty acres and a mule" policy after the Civil War, or how major universities, like Georgetown, respond to their use of slavery.

Many American adolescents do not realize the number of people in the world who can be considered slaves. Students can collect information for such websites as the Walk Free Foundation and the Antislavery. Such issues as forced marriages, human trafficking, child labor, and descent slavery are practiced in various countries around the world.

In 1938, the United States established the first version of the Fair Labor Standards Act. Students can study how the act has changed or not changed during the past eighty years. How does it relate to child labor laws? Is this act related to the discussion of minimum wages?

Students can research one of these related topics and begin to prepare an explanatory text that presents the issues as presented in explained in several sources and from several perspectives. This fits within the National Council of Teachers of English (NCTE) Standard 7 (1996). Students conduct research on issues and interests by generating ideas and questions, and by posing problems. They gather, evaluate, and synthesize data from a variety of sources (e.g., print and nonprint texts, artifacts, people) to communicate their discoveries in ways that suit their purpose and audience.

Research projects like this encourage students to extend their knowledge beyond the classroom and into the world in which they will be citizens. Individuals or groups of students can collect and analyze information that they can shape into explanatory essay on the issue.

The assignment can be structured in a way that the teacher can reinforce the writing process. While reading *To Be a Slave* (Lester & Feelings, 1968) and exploring the connected resource pages on their specific topic, students can do several moments of prewriting. Then, they can begin drafting, peer editing, and revision. After significant feedback, they can produce a complete rough draft that can be reviewed before producing a final draft for assessment and presentation.

All three activities—the visual discovery, the reading and preparing of information from the Slave Narratives, and the informational essay—are avenues to cross-curricular learning. A unit focused on *To Be a Slave* (Lester & Feelings, 1968) that extends into current issues helps students see how studying history helps contextualize current societal issues. The concerns of social justice problems can be connected to and/or be a result of past events. The goals of the #BlackLivesMatter movement or of kneeling during the star-spangled banner are related to America's history of slavery, and it is important to consider what questions we ask as we teach.

CONCLUSION

Julius Lester is one of the bright lights of YA literature from the beginning of the era until 2008, a forty-year period. Teachers and students will find his nonfiction enlightening and still relevant within the context of the current national debates on race and reparation for slavery. His fiction, while covering issues of race, also covers issues of family, identity, and young love. This chapter includes activities to help teachers engage students in research, writing, and analysis that can create in-depth discussions about history.

REFERENCES

Armstrong, W. H. (1969). *Sounder*. Austin: Holt, Rinehart and Winston.

Donelson, K. L., & Nilsen, A. P. (1980). *Literature for today's young adults*. Glenview, IL: Scott, Foresman.

Federal Writers' Project, & Botkin, B. A. (1945). *Lay my burden down; a folk history of slavery*. Chicago, IL: University of Chicago press.

Federal Writers' Project, & Botkin, B. A. (1946). *Lay my burden down; a folk history of slavery*. Chicago, IL: University of Chicago Press.

Hayes, A., Owens, S., & Simpson, D. J. (2010). *Bring learning alive!: Methods to transform middle and high school social studies instruction*. Palo Alto, CA: Teachers' Curriculum Institute.

Head, A. (1967). *Mr. and Mrs. Bo Jo Jones*. New York: Putnam.

Hinton, S. E. (1967). *The outsiders*. New York: Viking Press.

Ito, G. (2018). Julius Lester (1939–). Retrieved from https://www.blackpast.org/african-american-history/lester-julius-1939/

Lester, J. (1972). *Long journey home: Stories from Black history*. New York: Dial Press.

Lester, J., & Feelings, T. (1968). *To be a slave*. New York: Dial Press.

Lipsyte, R. (1967). *The contender*. New York: Harper & Row.

Medina, J. (2008). *Brain rules: 12 principles for surviving and thriving at work, home, and school* (1st ed.). Seattle, WA: Pear Press.

National Council of Teachers of English Urbana IL, National Council of Teachers of English Urbana IL, & International Reading Association Newark DE. (1996). *Standards for the English Language Arts*. S.l.: Distributed by ERIC Clearinghouse.

Nilsen, A. P., Blasingame, J., Donelson, K. L., & Nilsen, D. L. F. (2013). *Literature for today's young adults* (9th ed.). Boston: Pearson.

Potok, C. (1967). *The chosen; a novel*. New York: Simon and Schuster.

United States, Works Progress Administration, & Federal Writers' Project. (1937). Portraits of African American ex-slaves from the U.S. Works Progress Administration, Federal Writers' Project slave narratives collections [graphic].

Wilhelm, J. D. (2016). *You gotta BE the book: teaching engaged and reflective reading with adolescents* (3rd ed.). New York: Teachers College Press.

Williams, S. (2019, Feb. 25, 2019). Spike Lee's Oscar speech was a lesson in black history. Retrieved from https://www.vice.com/en_uk/article/d3m4jm/spike-lees-oscar-speech-was-a-lesson-in-black-history

Writers' Program (Va.). (1940). *The Negro in Virginia*. New York: Hastings House.

Zindel, P. (1968). *The pigman: A novel* (1st ed.). New York: Harper & Row.

Zindel, P. (1969). *My darling, my hamburger: A novel*. New York: Harper & Row.

Chapter 10

Racialized Constructions in the Stories by Mildred Taylor

Wanda Brooks and Desiree Cueto

I think Paul isn't free because even though he looks white, it fools the White people only until they find out that he is a Man of Color. He may receive some privileges, and because he looks white, some Whites still find out one way or the other that he isn't fully white. They still treat him like the rest of the colored people when it comes to rights and respect. . . . They would always see your color and not your personality. (Wesley, 8th grader)

Above, an African American 8th-grade adolescent grapples with fluid and contradictory historical distinctions around skin color, racial identity, racism, and white supremacy. Wesley's comments refer to a YA historical fiction story titled *The Land*. Although there are no "tragic mulattoes" (grappling with self-hatred), in Mildred Taylor's novel, young readers can contemplate and respond to the ambiguity and power of skin color as it relates to blacks, particularly those of a mixed racial identity like the protagonist Paul Edward Logan, living in the United States during the late 1800s.

The Land is one of a number of masterfully crafted and award-winning titles Mildred Taylor has written throughout the past forty years. In this chapter, after a summary and analysis of the novel, issues of defining and deconstructing race are taken up (Mahiri, 2017) followed by a brief overview of Taylor's staying power as an author. The chapter concludes with instructional guidance for teachers who wish to include this highly regarded novel in their English Language Arts classrooms.

THE LAND: DEPICTIONS OF MIXED RACED HERITAGE

As depicted by Taylor, Paul Edward Logan represents a visionary character. He is unafraid to embrace his mixed heritage despite the unavoidable racial

121

obstacles he faces in postbellum America. Taylor successfully complicates the history of Cassie Logan's family in *The Land*, via her examination of Paul Edward Logan's beginnings.

Paul Edward Logan and his sister Cassie are the product of a biracial African and Indian enslaved mother and a slave-owning father and plantation owner. Early on neither Cassie nor her younger brother is allowed to be confused by their identities—they are taught to ignore the underlying biological ties between a parent and child:

> Now, I always called my daddy "Mister Edward," just as Cassie and my mama did. . . . It seemed peculiar to me at first that I called my daddy a formal name while Robert and Hammond and George called him "Daddy." But my mama had broken both Cassie and me when we were still little from ever calling Edward Logan "Daddy." She had broken that misspeaking with bottom-warming spankings whenever we did. (Taylor, 2001, p. 41)

Irrespective of the guidance Paul received from his mother, he does go through a difficult stage of learning to navigate the racial boundaries located around his family members. Because Edward Logan insisted that his white sons (Robert, Hammond, and George) treat Paul as a brother and not property, Paul experiences confusion as he enters adolescence.

The dynamics found in Paul's family are unusual but not unheard of given the legacy of slavery in US history. Likewise, today, the racial heterogeneity among blacks in the United States stems from long-standing historical and geographic diasporic conditions. These conditions produced contexts in which black women found themselves willingly and, often, unwillingly producing off-spring with those from another race. In *Deconstructing Race*, Mahiri reflects on the legacy and instability of racial categories:

> In attempts to claim a more salient identity, people who have their DNA tested are almost always surprised, if not shocked, by rich, unrecognized diversity in their backgrounds. How complex and uniquely specified would an individual's identity be if it was informed by (reverse engineered by) direct connections to at least seven generations in the past? . . . Understanding human identity within a flow of generations further illuminates the false notions of racial purity that are central to the hierarchies of white supremacy. (2017, p. 25)

In many respects, Mr. Logan disrupts the familiar narrative about white supremacy and white men in postbellum America. He chooses to love, raise, and educate Cassie and Paul in close proximity to his white family, before and after the death of his white wife. Furthermore, the love that he demonstrates is a responsible love. Mr. Logan makes it very clear to everyone in his family that notwithstanding his own color-blindness, he is aware of the privileges he possesses and the disadvantages his son Paul will have to face:

All your life I've protected you. Don't you know that? But I just can't protect you in the same way I do Robert, George, and Hammond. I know how white men treat colored men, how white folks treat colored folks, and maybe I've been wrong in not making you understand earlier that the way I treat you is not the way every white man is going to treat you. (Taylor, 2001, p. 85)

Paul's mother has no illusions about the role she plays in the life of Edward Logan. She also understands that she is a black mother responsible for the safety and future of her children. Thus, from her perspective, it was very important that Paul learn that he has two families, one black and one white:

I been telling you and telling you those brothers of yours are white and you ain't. I been telling you that the day was gonna come when things wouldn't be the same between you and them. . . . I been telling you but you ain't been listening. . . . Now the day's come. Merry Christmas. (Taylor, 2001, p. 90)

Mitchell Thomas is the character who will prove to be more of a brother to Paul than any of his biological siblings. Mitchell is the black friend who runs away with Paul to achieve his dreams of owning land and an identity equal or greater to that of his father Edward Logan. Mitchell is the first character to explain to Paul how he is seen by others on and around his father's land. Mitchell explains to Paul that simply because of his white appearance, and the status of his father, Paul could expect to evoke hostility from his fellow blacks, intentional or not.

RACIAL HERITAGE CONFRONTS WHITE PRIVILEGE

Among other themes, Taylor's narrative (and subsequent novels) raises questions of why white people are threatened by the prospect of black people owning land. The narrative suggests that white identity is somehow put at risk by landowning blacks, even those who look white. It appears that land has the capacity to make manifest as well as destroy racial definition. For example, toward the conclusion of this narrative, Paul Logan learns that because he's been socially constructed as "black" (he will have no legal right to the land owned by his white father).

In other words, because of his racial heritage (African, European, and Indian American) Paul Edward Logan will not be allowed to share in his father's land or privilege. As a result, he must embark on a quest for his own piece of property. Because of the relentless labor invested by Paul and Mitchell (before Mitchell's death) the two men manage to clear an impossible amount of forest on a piece of land that will act as the down payment for Paul's dream.

After the work is done, however, Paul is cheated by the white landowner. Fortunately, after being swindled, Paul's sister is able to give him the land purchased by his mother to help secure his future. *The Land* has an almost idyllic ending with Paul and Mitchell's widow, Caroline, living happily ever after. Paul and Caroline eventually become the grandparents of Cassie Logan, the protagonist in Taylor's highly acclaimed 1976 Newbery Award novel, *Roll of Thunder, Here My Cry*.

TAYLOR'S STAYING POWER: HISTORICAL FICTION THAT FORESHADOWS CONTEMPORARY AMBIGUITIES ABOUT THE STABILITY AND FLUIDITY OF RACE

Although in different eras and told through the perspective of varied protagonists (young and old), the layers and complexities of race can be found throughout Taylor's entire body of work. For example, in *The Land*, at an early age (almost twelve years old), Paul Logan learns that his racial identity is something to be worn with caution and pride. As he gets older, Paul Logan develops a fully functional ability to see through the eyes of both the oppressor and the oppressed in this narrative.

Through his understanding and acceptance of his identity, Paul also learns that race does not have to define and in many cases confine his life. In other words, Paul Edward Logan is an extraordinary young man because he embodies and challenges readers to rethink views on race as articulated by Mahiri:

> Race is a socially constructed idea that humans can be divided into distinct groups based on inborn traits that differentiate them from members of other groups. This conception is core to practices of racism. (2017, p. 2)

Beyond *The Land*, Taylor's books all include characters grappling with race, racism, or white supremacy.

Taylor stands well ahead of her contemporaries in writing about these issues through her portrayal of multidimensional African American characters throughout the past four decades. When asked about representations of diversity in today's literature for youth, Taylor explained:

> There was a time when African-Americans were all "lumped together" as a group, and often stereotyped as a group. Today we are allowed to be as diverse as our nation, and writers must continue to address this diversity in order to portray "well-rounded" African-Americans. (Taylor, 2008)

Mildred Taylor received the NSK Neustadt prize for children's literature in 2003 for her entire body of work on the Logan Family. Prior to this, she'd won prestigious awards such as the Newbery Medal and the Coretta Scott

King Award. Furthermore, countless book reviews, literary analyses, and interviews have pointed to the significance of her writing and the importance of including her books in today's classrooms (Johnson, 2004).

PEDAGOGY

Taylor's body of work invites students to engage in critical inquiries about America's past and present. *The Land*, in particular, serves as an invitation to explore interconnections between identity, location, and power.

Individual Activity. *Environmental Autobiographies* or *Neighborhood Memory Maps*

Questions surrounding who we are, where we are from, and how these factors influence our lot in life are especially relevant to adolescents. Giving students the opportunity to grapple with these questions in relation to their own lives, as they consider Paul's evolving sense of self in *The Land*, should support deeper understanding of the book. We suggest two individual activities that invite students to use an excerpt from *The Land* (see following) as well as their own experiences and observations to refine their understanding of how place influences identity.

> I loved my daddy's land. In the beginning I always thought of it as my land too. I knew every bit of the place. I knew every bit of lowland, every rise and knoll, every cave and watering place, every kind of plant and tree. My favorite spots were the pond nestled in the woods and a hillside that overlooked the pasture and my daddy's house. The pond was surrounded by big old pines that allowed splinters of light to peek through, and its waters were filled with fish. The hillside boasted only a few trees, so it was sunny and open, and the pasture below was dotted with cows and horses grazing. On many days I would sit for hours alone at either place, just gazing out over the land. (p. 35)

Option 1: *Environmental Autobiographies*

Marcus (2014) writes about the connection between place and identity, noting that the two are co-produced. The environmental autobiography assignment begins with guided meditation. Teachers ask students to think about a place that has had a special meaning, a place with which they identify. Teachers then ask a series of questions while students visualize the place.

- What was the landscape? Colors? Textures?
- What was the atmosphere? Calm? Exciting? Frightening? Comfortable?
- What was the experience? Smell? Sound?

- What strong memories were created in the place? Who or what was there with you? What did you do there?

Going deeper, teachers ask students to consider how the places they inhabit become part of their identity. Students should reflect on how Paul's father's land shaped his identity and how excerpts from *The Land* inform their thinking about place and identity. Students will use this information to create an original narrative (oral, video, or written), which includes the following:

- A place that tells something about your identity.
- How or why does this place tell something about you?
- Three objects that you would find in this place.

OPTION 2: *NEIGHBORHOOD MEMORY MAPS*

In lieu of narrative writing, teachers might also consider asking students to draw neighborhood memory maps. Short (2012) finds that mapping memories allows students to explore the inscape of their cultural and personal identities. To support students' inquiries, teachers ask them to draw places in their neighborhoods that are significant to them. Their maps can be large or small, outdoors or indoors—their backyard, a room in their house, a city block or subdivision, a small town, a beach or forest area, and so forth.

Next, ask students to label the stories on their maps—the places where something happened that is a memory. Once completed, students place their maps on display, creating a gallery walk around the classroom. Students examine their classmates' maps and discuss similarities and differences in memories and maps across their classroom community.

SMALL-GROUP ACTIVITY:
PAIRED TEXTS AND *CONNECT, EXTEND, CHALLENGE*

In order to situate *The Land* in historical context and also examine the timelessness of its themes across the ages, teachers might consider selecting one or two paired-texts (e.g., a primary source document, speech, second novel or poem). For example, you might pair Paul's description of his racial identity with President, Barack Obama's "A More Perfect Union" speech, also known as the "Speech on Race," which was delivered during his 2008 presidential campaign.
Paul Logan:

I did have a white daddy. . . . My mama was called by the name of Deborah, and she was equally of the African people and of the native people, the Indians, whom we call the nation. She was a beautiful woman. My daddy took a liking to her soon after she came into womanhood, and that's how my sister Cassie and I came to be. Cassie and I were our daddy's children and both of us were born into slavery. Now, there are a lot of white men who fathered colored children in those days, even though the law said no white man could legally father a black child; that was in part so no child of color could inherit from his white daddy. (p. 11)

President Obama:

I am the son of a black man from Kenya and a white woman from Kansas. I was raised with the help of a white grandfather who survived a Depression to serve in Patton's Army during World War II and a white grandmother who worked on a bomber assembly line at Fort Leavenworth while he was overseas. I've gone to some of the best schools in America and lived in one of the world's poorest nations. I am married to a black American who carries within her the blood of slaves and slave-owners—an inheritance we pass on to our two precious daughters. I have brothers, sisters, nieces, nephews, uncles and cousins, of every race and every hue, scattered across three continents, and for as long as I live, I will never forget that in no other country on Earth is my story even possible. It's a story that hasn't made me the most conventional candidate. But it is a story that has seared into my genetic makeup the idea that this nation is more than the sum of its parts - that out of many, we are truly one.

After reading the two texts, which are thematically related, teachers can prompt students to consider how each piece connects to, extends, and challenges the other. An example of this visual thinking strategy is adapted in table 10.1.

Connect, Extend, Challenge works well with small groups, allowing students to keep a record of their ideas (Harvard Graduate School of Education, n.d.). Teachers might direct students' attention to the racial identity descriptions in both texts, ask students to share some of their thoughts and collect a list of ideas in each of the three categories. Additionally, teachers might want to push students' thinking about the reasons race was constructed by drawing their attention to Paul's remark "that was in part so no child of color could inherit from his white daddy" (p. 11).

Table 10.1 Visual Thinking Strategy

Connect	Extend	Challenge
How do the ideas, themes and information presented in the text CONNECT to each other?	EXTEND: What ideas, themes and information are EXTENDED or pushed in new directions as a result of reading the pair of texts?	CHALLENGE: How did the pair of texts CHALLENGE each other, or create space for critical thinking? What questions or wonderings do you now have?

Ask students to write their thoughts about the deeper meaning behind this remark on Post-it Notes and add them to a class chart to keep students' thinking alive over time. Teachers may use this exercise to encourage students to conduct research using additional texts and primary sources to learn about the topics related to race in America. Students might then categorize the texts and draw conclusions about the underlying reasons race was constructed.

- **Land ownership and voting rights:** In 1800, most states had restrictions on who was allowed to vote. States in the North and South gave the right to vote to white men who had a certain amount of property or wealth.
- **The one drop rule:** A principle of racial classification asserting that any person with even one ancestor of African ancestry, or a drop of black blood, is considered black.
- **Anti-miscegenation laws:** Laws that forbid interracial marriages.

As students' understanding about racial constructs develops, they should be encouraged to continually add new ideas and revisit the questions on the chart.

WHOLE-CLASS ACTIVITY: *CHARACTER ANALYSIS AND FINAL REFLECTIONS*

The Land invites an analysis of the processes through which social categories, roles, and practices are created, maintained, and transformed. Teachers might use a graphic organizer to help students think about broader themes related to power, and to map out the issues, the action, and clues about the character's agency that prompted him/her to take action. Assign groups of students different characters and ask each group to present its findings to create a multifaceted look at power, agency, and action (see table 10.2).

Reflection: When the character analysis is complete, students should have a chance to reflect on the entire book. What did they learn? About power?

Table 10.2   A multifaceted look at power, agency, and action

Title	Character(s)		Issue(s)	
The Land				
	Power		*Agency*	*Action*
What is within the character's control?	What is outside of the character's control?	What strengths or assets does the character possess?	What actions does the character take?	

About the issues? About agency? How has the book affected their under-standing of race or racial constructions? How do constructed notions of race play out today? What actions might be taken to challenge the validity of these ideas?

CONCLUSION

Mildred Taylor's body of work is perhaps most appreciated for its authentic-ity and honesty. Her writing bluntly exposes real issues in America's past and present. Readers leave *The Land* with a deeper understanding of how racial categorizations were used to justify brutality and injustice. At the same time, they learn that African Americans did not passively accept their plight but resisted the dehumanization of enslavement with wit and fortitude.

REFERENCES

Harvard Graduate School of Education. (n.d.) Visible thinking. Retrieved from http://www.pz.harvard.edu/projects/visible-thinking

Johnson, D. (2004). A tribute to Mildred Taylor. *World Literature Today,* May–Aug, p. 4.

Mahiri, J. (2017). *Deconstructing Race: Multicultural Education beyond the Color-Bind.* New York, NY: Teachers College Press.

Marcus, C. C. (2014). Environmental Autobiography. *Room One Thousand,* 2. Retrieved from https://escholarship.org/uc/item/1rr6730h

Obama, B. (2008, March). A more perfect union. Speech presented in Philadel-phia, PA. https://constitutioncenter.org/amoreperfectunion/docs/Race_Speech_Transcript.pdf

Short, K. (2012) Neighborhood memory maps: Language and culture book kits & global story boxes. Worlds of words. Retrieved from http://create arizona.org/curricular-experiences/story-interactions/storyresources/neighbor hood-memory-map

Taylor, M. (2008). [Interview]. Retrieved from https://thebrownbookshelf.com/28days/mildred-taylor/

BIBLIOGRAPHY OF MILDRED TAYLOR'S WORKS

Song of the Trees (1975)
Roll of Thunder, Hear My Cry (1976)
Let the Circle Be Unbroken (1981)

The Gold Cadillac (1987)
The Friendship (1987)
Mississippi Bridge (1990)
The Road to Memphis (1992)
The Well: David's Story (1995)
The Land (2001)

Editor and Author Biographies

Steven T. Bickmore is an associate professor of English education at UNLV and maintains a weekly academic blog on YA literature (http://www.yawednesday.com/). He is a past editor of *The ALAN Review* (2009–2014) and a founding editor of *Study and Scrutiny: Research in Young Adult Literature*.

Wanda M. Brooks is an associate professor in the Department of Teaching and Learning at Temple University. She coordinates all of the middle-grade teacher certification programs in the College. She teaches courses related to literacy theories, research, and instruction as well as qualitative research methods.

Shanetia P. Clark, PhD, is an associate professor of literacy in the Department of Early and Elementary Education at Salisbury University in Salisbury, Maryland. Her interests include young adult and children's literature, the exploration of aesthetic experiences within reading and writing classrooms, and writing pedagogy.

Chris Crowe is a former high school English teacher who is now a professor of English at Brigham Young University, where he teaches YA literature and creative writing. A longtime member of ALAN, he has also served on its board of directors and as president in 2001–2002. He has published books and articles including *Mississippi Trial, 1955* and the nonfiction book *Getting Away with Murder: The True Story of the Emmett Till Case.*

M. Cathrene Connery, PhD, is an associate professor of literacy and children's literature at Salisbury University in Salisbury, Maryland. A bilingual educator, researcher, and advocate, she has drawn on Vygotskian theory to inform her research and professional activities in language, literacy, and sociocultural studies.

Desiree Cueto is an assistant professor in the Department of Elementary Education at Western Washington University. She is the director of the Pacific Northwest Children's Literature Clearinghouse and teaches courses in children's literature and language arts methods. She also serves as chair of the NCTE Charlotte Huck Award for Outstanding Fiction for Children and is a section editor for the *AERA Handbook of Research on Teachers of Color*.

Cheryl Logan is a lecturer and a PhD student at the Ohio State University. Her research interests include African and African American YA literature, and representations of black boyhood and fatherhood. She teaches courses on diversity, multiculturalism, children's and YA literature, and methods in language arts to undergraduates and preservice teachers.

Ruth McKoy Lowery is a professor of children's literature and literacy, and interim chair of the Department of Teaching and Learning at the Ohio State University. Her current research focuses on immigrant and multicultural literature, the adaptation of immigrant and at-risk students in schools, and preparing teachers to teach a diverse student population.

Ngozi Onuora is chair for the African American Studies minor and associate professor in the School of Education at Millikin University. She teaches children's literature, language arts methods, and reading methods. Her research interests include portrayals of female slaves in literature for middle-grade readers, depictions of the American Civil War in nonfiction for middle-grade readers, and multicultural representation in graphic novels for young adults.

Deborah Taylor recently retired from the Enoch Pratt Free Library in Baltimore, MD. She has chaired and served on many ALA committees, including the 2015 Sibert Award for Outstanding Informational Books for Children, the Newbery Awards, Coretta Scott King Book Awards, and the Printz Award. She was named the 2015 recipient of the Coretta Scott King/Virginia Hamilton Award for Lifetime Achievement.

Nancy D. Tolson is the assistant director of the African American Studies Program at the University of South Carolina. Thanks to her parents, she acquired a strong interest in black literature and culture. As a Fulbright Fellow, Nancy spent a year as a research/lecturer in Cape Coast, Ghana, researching folklore and teaching Elementary Education courses at the University of Cape Coast.